DREGS ISLAND

WRITTEN BY

DR. BON BLOSSMAN

and

ZAKK MYER

Create Space Publishing, USA
First Paperback Edition: April 2017

Blossman, Bon 1970— Myer, Zakk 1995—
Dregs Island / by Dr. Bon Blossman and Zakk Myer
Summary: Seventeen-year-old Alex Cardin is falsely convicted of a felony. It is six years after President Gray's Prison Reform Act of 2026. Prisons have been shut down across the United States, and all felons must serve life sentences on isolated prison islands where escape is impossible, and rules of civility are obsolete. Alex is banished to Dregs Island and must rely on his sharp intuition, as nobody can be trusted. To survive, he must defeat the ruthless ruler of the island who was a legendary serial killer back on the mainland. Alex is forced to make decisions along the way that weigh survival against humankind and family against friendship.

ISBN: 0-9965248-3-5
ISBN-13: 978-0-9965248-3-4
[1. Dystopia - Fiction. 2. Thriller – Fiction. 3. Action – Fiction. 4. Prisons – Fiction. 5. Adventure – Fiction.]

CONTENTS

Justice finds a way.

ACKNOWLEDGMENTS

A special thanks to Jason Myer for the cover art, and to Eric Blossman for the book trailer soundtrack. It means the world to us to have such talented, amazing, and supportive members of our family.
Zakk would also like to acknowledge his girlfriend, Alex, for being his #1 fan.

1 BLACK SEDAN

Across the intersection, a white-haired woman in a pink dress leaned against a pole on the corner as she waited for the crosswalk. My foot rested on the brake as I gazed at the cloudless Odessa sky, begging the Texas heat for mercy. A black sedan appeared in my rearview mirror, inching closer with haste. The traffic light beamed red, but the car accelerated as the lady's orthopedic shoes connected with the road. With her eyes forward, she hobbled onto the street, making her way to the other side. The driver swerved into the adjacent lane with a shrill screech. Nearly choking on air, I gasped as it sprang into the crossing without as much of a brake flicker.

I rolled down my window to scream at the lady in pink, as my other hand compelled the horn. She swiveled her head toward me just as the car struck her, catapulting her body into the air before it smacked against the hot pavement, bouncing twice before tumbling into a final position. The car's engine roared as it accelerated, disappearing into the distance.

"GLC889. GLC889. GLC889," I repeated aloud, grabbing my phone to make a voice note, so I didn't forget. "GLC889. Black Lincoln Town Car. Texas plates."

I threw my shifter in park, not bothering to kill the engine, and hurried across the road to render aid. The only breeze was that from the run, and the relentless sun seared my scalp. Burned rubber hung thickly in the air with hints of powdery perfume and copper of freshly spilled blood. There were no cars around. There was no one on the sidewalks. My throat constricted, and my body's core turned to ice. Nothing of this magnitude had ever crossed my path before. As I marched over to her discarded marionette doll figure, I surveyed the broken limbs and lacerations dispersed across her creped skin. With her chest massacred upon impact, crimson stains had soaked into the front of her dress like a Rorschach image. Blood seeped from her skull, thickening as it cooked on the boiling concrete. Her head faced me with widened eyes, projected at a ninety-degree angle to her body. No need to search for vitals. She was gone.

With my chest heaving, I dialed 9-1-1. The operator answered within seconds, but it seemed like an eternity. I cleared my throat.

"There's been a hit and run, license plate GLC889, a black Lincoln Town Car. A woman's dead. I'm at East University Boulevard and Golder Avenue. My name's Alex Cardin. I'm only seventeen. I don't know what to do. Please help."

The voice on the other end of the line instructed me to move out of the street, out of harm's way. Something deep inside wouldn't allow me to leave her body there, so I kneeled by the crumpled corpse. Approaching motorists became confused by my parked car at the stoplight and the woman on the ground. Cars pulled over to the side of the road, and a crowd soon gathered. With gaped jaws, onlookers raised their mobile devices to record the scene, but nobody offered assistance. After hanging up with 9-1-1, my adrenaline directed traffic until the police arrived.

Minutes had passed before the sirens rang in the distance and red-and-blue swirling lights arrived on scene. I moved to the side of the street as an ambulance pulled next to the body and parked.

"What'd you do, son?" a bald man in a tracksuit asked as he raised his phone to film me.

A lady in a business suit stepped closer with a smirk on her face.

"Ha! You know exactly what he did. He was probably texting a girl or checking himself in the mirror. Guys like that care about one thing, you know."

"It wasn't me. A black sedan hit her and drove away."

Disturbed by the bystanders, I jogged over to tell my story to the paramedics. They ignored me as if I was invisible as they yanked equipment from the back of their truck. Like robots, they had a job to do, a strict, programmed protocol, but their efforts were futile. Pulling out gadgets from their bags, they rushed to the victim, checking for vital signs. Not one of us needed a day of medical training to see her demise was more than obvious.

A middle-aged peace officer, with messy hair and wide-set eyes, hopped out of his cruiser and sauntered toward the victim with a scowl on his face. I sighed, realizing the driver of the sedan had had far too much time to evade the scene. The policeman was in no hurry as he glanced at the woman before heading toward me.

"You hit her?" he asked as he pulled out a pen from his front pocket.

"No, sir. I reported the plate number to the 9-1-1 operator. The guy that hit her left the scene."

"Please give me your driver's license."

I fumbled to retrieve my identification from my wallet.

"Alright, I'll need you to sit right over there, be back in a minute," the officer said, as he turned toward his black-and-white.

"My car's over there. I'll move it," I said as I pointed to my Honda Civic at the stoplight.

"You can't just leave your car parked at an intersection. You're blocking a lane, young man," he said, pausing to scribble my license plate on his form. "I can issue a ticket for vehicle abandonment and reckless driving."

"What? Are you serious? I was trying to help that woman."

"Really? Trying to help her? Nobody can save that sack of skin. She's not in need of aid. She needs a coroner. Move your vehicle to that lot, and wait on the curb," he said, pointing across the street at an office parking garage.

Without another word, I pulled my car into the garage. "What the hell?" I mumbled, trying not to stare at the cop as he wrote on his clipboard. He grabbed the radio from his shoulder as I pulled into a parking space. *Dammit!* Upon seeing the groceries in the backseat I had bought for my mother, I cringed and checked the time. I sent her a text message to tell her I would be a few minutes late.

After taking a seat on the pavement across from the victim's body, I waited in silence, watching the medics peel the woman from the street and place her carcass inside of a body bag. The bystanders glared at me as if I was a pariah. The policeman sat in his car with the engine running as he spoke to someone on his radio. *What was I waiting for? Wasn't I a Good Samaritan? Is this what doing the right thing feels like?*

An hour had passed, and my clothes were drenched from the burning sun. I had just texted my mother with a white lie about an after school study group so she wouldn't worry. As the cop approached, I raised my head, squinting at him.

"You have the right to remain silent. If you do say—"

"What? Are you arresting me? This—"

"If you do say anything, what you say can be used against you in a court of law. Stand up, young man," he said, as he flashed a pair of handcuffs in front of me.

Nausea flushed through my core, as I complied with jellied legs. The crowd of spectators jeered and shouted obscenities. With a hard blink of my eyes to remain conscious, I wiped the sweat from my face onto my shoulder. I jabbed my thumb into the side of my thigh, hoping to wake up, as I tried to convince myself it was just a nightmare.

"You have the right to consult with a lawyer. One will be appointed for you if you so desire."

A lady wearing scrubs poked me in the shoulder and grinned.

"Oh, the prison boys are gonna love your muscles. It's a shame what they'll do to your gorgeous face. Those beautiful brown eyes will be black and blue, and those pearly whites are good as gone."

"There are no more prisons, lady. He's going to the island. He's got no chance," a man standing beside her said.

The officer yanked my arm behind my back, and the merciless metal of the restraints slammed against my flesh. He tightened the cuff around each wrist until it could no longer produce another click. As he escorted me to his car, the growing mob of pedestrians followed with phones raised.

"I didn't do it, sir. You have to believe me. I saw who did it."

"Get in," he said, shoving me into the backseat.

The car door slammed shut.

2 SWIFT JUSTICE

The iron gate crashed into place with a deafening boom. The air was thin and saturated with a vile mold. I didn't belong there. Three concrete slabs with a barrier of reinforced bars - no place for a recent high school graduate. I hadn't had enough time on Earth to develop a career, a craft, or even to find my purpose. The cell harbored shrouds of shadow, the only light in the room streamed in fragmented rays from a grungy corridor. My new roommates rested in bunk beds against the walls - some mumbling from drunken stupors and others so still they might have been dead. My hands wrapped around the railing of a cold, steel ladder, and an angry face glared at me from below, sizing me up as if I were his next meal. Climbing to the top bed, I mused about how the justice system had failed me, the victim, and her family. It didn't make sense that everyone at the scene assumed I was guilty. I had always seen in movies that you could call someone if you were arrested, but they never gave me the opportunity and even took my phone. As they processed me into the jail, nobody had spoken a word, and not one person would listen to my story. It was maddening. *I'll never leave the house again if I get out of this mess.*

My feet hung off the edge of the thin mattress, so I folded my knees until I fit. I shook out a flimsy blanket and flung a massive spider onto my chest. The darkened room morphed the creature into a shadowy figure of eight gangly legs that took turns elongating as if I had awoken him and he needed to stretch. The creepy beast flew into the air as I swiped at it while suppressing an irrational freak out. In attempts at blending in with my environment, I slid the cover on top of my neon-orange jumpsuit. However, I couldn't help but run my fingers across the fleece to check for members of his family. An icy stream of air howled through the overhead vents above my head, killing any chance of sleep. Graffiti created by villains past covered the concrete blocks lining the back wall of my bunk. At least I had something to keep my brain occupied.

"Whaddya in fer?" a deep voice echoed from the dark corner.

Slow, muted footsteps approached, and a shagged beard emerged from the shadows. With a gulp, I mustered a response as his face leveled with mine.

"I-I don't know."

He snorted.

"Now that's the funniest thing I heard all week! Me name's Joe," he said in a pirate-like manner with a grim smile.

Unaware of jail cell rules, I hesitated in an awkward silence before I whispered in response.

"Nice to meet you, Joe."

He cocked his head to the side, and I could barely discern a grin through his thick beard.

"Ye prob'ly thinks me's a criminal, but me's not."

I stared at the ceiling vent until my eyes stung from the cold air.

"Well, I didn't think you—"

"Ye prob'ly thinks me done killed someone."

"Um, no, no I don't."

Please go away. I recoiled under the pilled blanket. My eyes darted around the cell, anticipating others to join in and take the attention off me.

"Call me fren. That's all me wants."

"Okay, I'll call your friend. What's his name? How would I reach him?"

I pressed against my chest to slow my heart, taking in a calming breath of the fusty air.

"No. No. No. Ye call me fren." He dwelled on the moment with a crooked smile before unleashing a raucous laugh. "Look, me's not tryna hurt a good fella like yerself. Me just wants t' be yer fren."

My primal brain ordered the production of copious tears and a cry out for my mother. I was thankful my survival drive kept the sobbing at bay and suspended all movement. I held my breath and tightened my shoulders as Joe stepped closer, narrowing the space between us. He had a roaming eye that gave him a permanently distracted look. A new scenario in my repertoire, I turned into a deer caught in the headlights.

"Joe, please—"

"Call me fren."

My eyes burned a hole into my blanket until a chipper whistle rang from the hallway. Within seconds, a muscled guard waltzed by the jail cell twirling a stick.

"Please, help!"

The moment the words left my lips, I regretted my outburst as the footsteps halted. The correctional officer wore the standard khaki uniform with a thick utility belt holding various weapons. His blond hair was short and spiked, and he had dark eyebrows in an arch like a pop star. Through the bars, he searched for the owner of the voice. In the grim darkness, he widened a smile.

"Well, you've already helped yourself by getting in there, Alexander Cardin. You're in good hands now." He chuckled. "I see you've made *a friend*."

A moment of silence had beset the room before he swished off through the corridor. *Why the hell did I do that?* With my heart edging up my throat, I scrambled to establish an action plan for when the giant murderous freak launched an attack.

"Got cig'rettes on ye?" the pirate asked, his foul breath coating my nostrils.

In a state of confusion, I propped up on an elbow and explored the room with my eyes for movement. *Why wasn't Joe angry I called for help? Why did nobody react?* As I locked into a gaze with Joe, I realized he reminded me of a serial killer – one who had worn a clown mask and hacked people with a machete in their beds. I suddenly didn't mind the chilly air, as my core was heating up like a barbecue grill.

"No. Um, I don't smoke."

I swallowed a hard lump as I flattened against the mattress.

"Ima have t'check."

I paralyzed every fiber of my being as Joe patted me down like a TSA agent, my eyes fixed on the ceiling vent and doing everything I could to avoid eye contact.

"So, what are you in here for, Joe?"

I said the first thing that came to mind, as I needed a distraction.

"Murder." He paused and waited for my reaction. I stayed frozen with a blank expression. "Don' worry, me don' kill ev'yone, jus' t'bad ones."

As I expected. I would have done anything to get the creep to leave me alone, but he stood still, staring at me as if I was his favorite television show.

"So, do you kill them with a knife? A gun? How does that work?"

The unprocessed words spewed from my rogue tongue, leading me down a terrible pathway.

"No need, gots me fists," he said as he smiled, flashing his enormous hands with battered knuckles.

I exhaled in slow increments. Joe turned abruptly and ambled back into the depths of the shadows.

The blond guard made his rounds once again, nightstick spinning in the air as he smacked gum like a junior high girl. Without moving a muscle, I waited for him to announce my release and tell me it was all a mistake. Instead, he approached the cell and clanked on the bars with his baton. I cringed, not wanting him to wake up more of my cellmates.

"How are you doing, Joe? Why'd you leave your new *friend*?"

Silence.

"Not the talkative type, huh? Or, do you just prefer to speak to young boys?" the officer said with a warped grin. "Mr. Cardin?"

My heart paused at the sound of my name.

"Yes, sir."

"Come with me. You have a visitor."

Skipping the bunk's ladder, I hurdled out of my bed and scurried out of the cell. The guard slammed the gate behind me and signaled to follow him. With eyes forward, I avoided what I imagined were pairs of hungry eyes glued to me from within the line of cells of the grim passageway. After navigating through a shabby maze, we walked up to a green door with a tiny window. The officer flung it open and shoved me into a room with a thick glass partition reinforced with bars, a red vintage telephone at each station. I spotted my brother.

"Tony," I yelled as I rushed toward an orange plastic chair at one of the stations.

I picked up the bulky receiver, staring at an expression of horror on the face that doubled as my reflection. We favored each other as twins but were eleven months apart in age. At five-foot-eleven, I was slightly taller, but he often boasted about being more athletic.

"What happened, Alex? Mom's so upset, she's doing what she can to find a lawyer, but she's having trouble finding anybody who will take the case without being paid."

"I witnessed a hit and run. I called in the license plate, but nobody did anything. Nobody cared, and the cop arrested *me*. Nothing makes sense."

"What's the license plate? That would be great to tell the attorney if we can ever get one."

Tony grabbed a pen and paper from the desk in front of him.

"GLC889. Black Lincoln Town Car. Texas plates." He scribbled on the pad. "Tony, it's very strange, but nobody cared I knew the car that hit the woman. It's like they pretended not to hear me."

The door behind me squealed as it opened. The guard glared at me and shot a coy smile at Tony.

"Let's go. Your trial's in the morning, at 6 AM, you better get some rest. You're lucky I allowed you a visitor outside of hours."

Tony ripped the paper from the pad and slid it into his pocket. A guard with short dreadlocks closed in on him.

"Trial? What do you mean there's a trial?" I said as Tony rose from his chair, his fists clenched white as he held onto the table and stared into my eyes.

"President Gray's Prison Reform Act of 2026 sped up the archaic judicial process. Nobody has to wait months or even years to know their fate anymore. Where've you been, man? I will admit a twenty-four-hour turnaround is the fastest I've seen. There must be a ton of evidence in your case," the blond guard said.

"No. No trial. I need to get out of here!"

"Yeah, you and everybody else," the guard said with a sour frown. "Let's go, Alexander Cardin. Now."

Tony banged his fist against the tabletop as he shirked away from the dreadlocked guard's grip.

" Alex, I won't give up, we will fix this if it's the last thing I do."

3 THE VERDICT

Seconds after sunbeams trickled down the corridor, a large pale man wearing a khaki uniform opened the gate.

"Alexander Cardin. Time to go."

"Um, am I going to be able to speak to a lawyer? I've been thinking about this trial being so quick, well, I –"

"That way." He pointed toward a sharp corner down a thin hallway. "That all changed in 2026."

I was only eleven that year. It was now 2032. Video games had been all that mattered to me. *What happened in 2026?* After two more turns, we ended at a dead-end facing a wooden door with many deadbolts. A UV light blinked from the ceiling, buzzing like a bug zapper. The guard disengaged the locks with a few different keys and escorted me into a large courtroom with an overpowering scent of lemon cleaner. My mother sobbed as she hunched over the front bench behind a waist-high partition. She was wearing the same baby blue dress she had just worn at my high school graduation, with her dark, prematurely gray-streaked hair in an unkempt bun. I locked eyes with her as she raised her head. My brother clambered to his feet as I marched across the room. With a quivering chin, he held back tears and shrugged his shoulder.

"Hello, Mr. Alexander Cardin, sit down."

A thin middle-aged man in a brown plaid suit was perched at a long wooden table. He gestured for me to take a chair beside him. I followed orders from the skinny man as I gawked like a three-year-old at his long, bony nose resembling a Pixar villain. We faced a large wooden wall with a massive gold seal in the center that read *Justice for All* with two American flags positioned on either side. A thickset man in a black robe sat on a high throne underneath the seal, glaring at the paperwork in front of him with pinched brows. He wore black-rimmed glasses that rested on his pudgy cheeks. A clock ticked on the wall to his right. 5:55 AM.

"Are you my attorney?"

"Yes, Mr. Cardin. My name is Roger Smalls, your court-appointed representative."

The man's lanky fingers fumbled for my file in his battered briefcase. I anticipated a lively soundtrack to play in my subconscious every time he made a move or spoke.

"But, shouldn't I have time to prepare my defense? I was wrongfully arrested yesterday afternoon. I witnessed a hit and run—"

He raised a palm to silence me.

"That's how things used to be, but as you well know, President Gray made many changes with that prison reform years ago. The courts retain the right to expedited trials when the evidence is overwhelming – such as where there are two or more eyewitnesses to a crime. The state just doesn't have the funding or the room for inmates anymore. Prisons across the country were closed down. Just last year, the last remaining prison in New York City was turned into a military academy. President Gray has nearly resolved our national debt, you know. Mr. Cardin, everything will be okay. I know what I'm doing. I've read your file, and your innocence is obvious."

"Pssst," a voice resonated behind me.

The chair creaked as I twisted around and joined a gaze with Tony. His face was panic-stricken.

"Mom couldn't raise funds in time, Alex. The bank doesn't open until 8 AM. She was going to get the money from the mortgage, but there's not time. We've tried absolutely everything. Ask if your appointed guy can postpone this thing." His voice wavered with emotion.

"Tony, it's okay. This is just a formality. There's no need to reschedule. He said it'll be alright. There's overwhelming evidence I'm not guilty and a couple of witnesses. That's why I'm getting a quick trial. They've figured out it's a misunderstanding. This is all for legal reasons. I think they call it red tape or something like that."

Tony gave a cautious smile.

"Ah, I understand. Good news. I'll tell Mom."

He scurried back to his seat to console my mother and relay the good news. The clock struck six o'clock, and the judge slammed his gavel on the desk.

"All rise," a petite female bailiff resembling Lucille Ball announced.

The judge glowered at me as I rose from my chair. His eyes were black as night.

"Department One of the Superior Court is now in session. The Honorable Judge Walter Glasgow is presiding. Please be seated."

The bailiff folded her arms across her chest. Shooting Tony a nervous glance before I took my seat, I inhaled a deep breath. Every cell in my body was a jittery mess as I sat motionless in my chair while the judge took the time to make deliberate eye contact with each person seated in the front. I was last in line, but he skipped me and addressed the court. This soured my stomach.

"Good morning, ladies and gentlemen. Calling the case of the People of the State of Texas versus Alexander Cardin. Are both sides ready?"

"Ready for the People, Your Honor," a man across the aisle said with confidence exuding from his pores.

The man who spoke was the district attorney. He wore a black suit with a metallic sheen and a bold, red tie. His hair was slicked back and black as coal.

"Ready for the defense, Your Honor," my attorney said in a tiny voice.

My mother moaned from the bench behind me as Tony whispered for her to be quiet.

"One more outburst and you will be removed from the courtroom."

Judge Glasgow aimed a chubby finger at my mother. Tony tried to calm her as she pressed both hands against her mouth, tears streaming from her puffy eyes. She nodded at me before bowing her head in an apology.

The district attorney cleared his throat. "Your Honor, the defendant is charged with the crime of vehicular homicide. The evidence shows that a 2001 Honda Civic, registered to Ms. Paula Cardin and driven by the defendant, was used to commit murder on August 7, 2032, at 4:34 PM at the intersection of East University Boulevard and Golder Avenue. The evidence I present proves the defendant is guilty as charged."

Vehicular homicide? Evidence? Against me? How could that be possible? My attorney rose to address the judge. I lowered my head to gaze at the floor and noticed he was wearing blue sneakers. An ominous sign – if the man didn't care enough to dress appropriately for court, he certainly wasn't prepared for my case.

"Your Honor, under the law, my client is presumed innocent until proven guilty. During this trial, you will hear no real evidence against my client. You will come to know the truth: that there was another car involved in the accident that left the scene. Um," he mumbled, pausing to sort through papers. He dropped a few papers on the floor. After bending over to pick them up, a chunk of hairspray-coated hair on the top of his head stood erect. "Mr. Cardin was only acting to assist the victim. Therefore, my client is not guilty."

That sounded reasonable. I inhaled a calming breath. The judge lowered his head onto the table, reading papers in front of him.

"The prosecution may call its first witness."

"The People call Mr. Quinton Smith."

The small bailiff walked by our table and smirked at my attorney's hair. She met a short man with bushy white hair at the waist-high gate. He wore a peach button-down shirt with fresh sweat stains around his armpits. I didn't recognize him. After escorting him to the witness stand, she instructed him to place his hand on a scroll of the United States Constitution.

"Raise your right hand. Do you promise that the testimony you shall give in this case before the court shall be the truth, the whole truth, and nothing but the truth?"

The man cast an impish grin at the judge who nodded in return, sliding his glasses back on his nose with an index finger. I shot a glance of concern to my attorney. He kept his eyes on the witness, the rogue chunk of hair on his head still standing at attention.

"I do."

"You may be seated."

The tiny guard scurried off to her place by the judge's bench, puckering her glossy red lips.

"Where do you work, Mr. Smith?" the DA asked, as he tapped on his podium.

"I work for the City, at the Water Department."

"What is the address of your place of employment?"

"102 Golder Avenue."

"Were you working on the day of August 7, 2032?"

"Yes."

"Did you happen to witness an accident?"

"Yes."

"Can you please describe for the court what you witnessed?"

He wiped the sweat from his brow with his shirtsleeve.

"In my office, there's a window facing Golder Avenue. I heard tires squealing, looked out the window, and witnessed a silver Honda Civic hitting an old lady in a pink dress. The driver then backed up his car to the stoplight at the intersection, parked it there, and got out of the car with a phone to his ear."

"Is the man who struck the woman with a Honda Civic in this courtroom?"

"Yes."

"Can you point out who hit Ms. Thelma Sterns with the silver Honda Civic at the intersection of East University Boulevard and Golder Avenue on August 7, 2032, at 4:34 PM?"

The witness raised his hand toward my table and pointed an index finger in my direction.

"Yes, it was that guy, the defendant."

The man's attention remained focused on the district attorney, and he never even looked at me. My eyelids widened until I thought my eyeballs would pop out of their orbits. My lungs made a funny raspy noise as I huffed for air.

"He's lying. There is no way he saw that because it didn't happen. It's not true," I said to Roger Smalls. My attorney kept his eyes on the witness.

The bailiff leaned over to the court reporter. "The

record will show that the witness has identified the defendant sitting at the defense table."

"Does the defense have any questions?" the judge said to my attorney.

"Not at this time, Your Honor."

My mother wailed as Tony quieted her.

"Please escort her out of the courtroom at once, bailiff."

Judge Glasgow scowled at my mother through his black-rimmed glasses as his cheeks flushed. The miniature Lucille Ball marched over to the benches and instructed my mom to exit the courtroom. My mother released an ear-splitting shriek before disputing the testimony in an indecipherable diatribe.

"If you do not exit the courtroom, Miss, you will be arrested for contempt of court," the judge shouted.

From my seat, I begged her to follow orders, asking Tony for help. My brother stood up to peel her off the bench, before cradling her slumped shoulders. A different guard approached from the back of the courtroom and escorted them out as her wails filled the room.

"Why do you not want to ask this man any questions? He's lying!" I said, my eyes burning with disgust.

"The witness is excused," the judge said.

Roger Smalls gawked at the judge, ignoring my pleas.

"The People call Officer Mike Chapman," the DA said with a slight upturn at the corners of his mouth.

With a raised hand and the other on the scroll, the

officer that had arrested me was sworn in before lowering himself onto the seat at the witness stand. The DA sprung to his feet, his narrowed eyes crinkling into a smile. I was confident this officer didn't have evidence against me, as he hadn't been present during the accident.

"Were you on duty the afternoon of August 7, 2032?"

The officer blinked repeatedly and cleared his throat a few times.

"Yes, I was patrolling the west side of downtown between Loop 338 and North Grandview Avenue."

"Did you observe a silver Honda Civic that afternoon?"

He underwent an unnatural pause, placing his index finger across his mouth and his thumb on his chin.

"Yes, I did."

"What was the license number?"

"982BIM."

"Where did you first see the car?"

After a slow swallow, he pulled on his lower lip with his teeth.

"I arrived on the scene only seconds after the homicide had taken place. I saw the Honda Civic where the defendant had moved it after hitting and killing Ms. Sterns. It was parked facing north on Golder at the stoplight of East University Boulevard and Golder Avenue."

"Did you speak to the defendant?"

The officer fidgeted in his chair and took a few

seconds to adjust his shirt cuffs under his jacket.

"Yes, I spoke to Alexander Cardin. He confessed to hitting the victim. Mr. Cardin explained he was voice-messaging his mother, Ms. Paula Cardin, and drove through the stoplight."

"That is a lie!" I said as I stood up.

Judge Glasgow glared at my attorney.

"Mr. Smalls, you need to counsel your client on how to behave in a courtroom."

"Listen to the 9-1-1 tapes! I reported the car that hit that lady. I didn't do it! This is all lies! GLC889. Black Lincoln Town Car. Texas plates."

"The court reporter will strike Mr. Cardin's eruption from the record. Mr. Smalls, I will give your client one more warning before I have him arrested for contempt of court - in addition to the serious charges he faces this morning."

"Mr. Cardin, do not say another word," Roger Smalls said, avoiding eye contact.

"Does the defense have any questions for the arresting officer?" the judge said.

"Not at this time, Your Honor."

My attorney gathered the papers in front of him and slipped them into a manila file folder. He bent over to slip the file into his tattered briefcase on the floor beside his feet. As he sat back up, the chunk of hair that was previously erect had filed back into place.

"The witness is excused," Judge Glasgow said, scribbling on the papers in front of him.

After a few minutes of silence, the bailiff accepted a

document from the judge and took a few steps forward. "Please stand, the judge has reached a verdict in the People of the State of Texas versus Alexander Cardin."

Mr. Smalls asked me to stand. My body was weak, and I leaned against the table to keep my knees from trembling.

"I find the defendant, Mr. Alexander Cardin, guilty of vehicular homicide. According to the Prison Reform Act of 2026, all felonious individuals will be banished from the United States of America and sentenced to live out their days on a prison island no less than 500 nautical miles from the border. Without further delay, Mr. Cardin will be processed and transported to Dregs Island. This concludes the People of the State of Texas versus Alexander Cardin. We thank you all for coming today."

4 TRANSPORT SHIP

Subtle boat rocking triggered a wave of nausea as the perspiration from my palms soaked into the hard birch wood of my seat. A bouquet of rat feces and biological decay coated the air. I twisted my limbs to find comfort within the heavy shackles. *How did this happen to me?* All hopes and dreams of finding my way in this world had vanished in less than twenty-four hours. My mother had already secured loans for my first semester of business school, yet I may never enter a college classroom. I pondered about what law meant without justice as I studied the seven other faces – a few with bleeding wounds, five males, and two females. Strapped to the benches like animals in chains, they all wore neon-orange jumpsuits like me.

Something creaked from above – a door. A campaign of footsteps rumbled, and within seconds, soldiers donning blue camouflage uniforms and clutching assault rifles marched down the stairs and into the vast space of the ship's bilge.

"I'm starving. Are you guys going to feed us?" a lanky prisoner with a wrinkled face and deep-set eyes said.

The largest guard, who remained by the staircase,

gave an icy stare. A ruddy-skinned soldier approached and, without saying a word, removed the restraints from the man's hands and feet as another guardsman with a black beard pressed his firearm against his chest. They both took a step back, and allowed the weak man to stand.

"So, am I finally going to get something to eat or what?"

The prisoner rose to his feet, balancing as the boat rocked. The ruddy-skinned officer struck him with his fist in the temple, and he plummeted to the ground, moaning. Two more guards joined into the melee, pummeling him with the butt of their rifles as sprays of blood spewed from his body. After a few minutes of the officers kicking the man with their combat boots, the inmate's body went limp, and the moaning ceased. His body was sprawled out on the wooden floor, oozing scarlet streams from his face. The bearded guard stepped up holding his rifle like a golf club. He took a swing at the man's head and connected with his skull. The bones fractured as easy as an eggshell, his bare blood-coated brain glistened in the sun.

"One down, seven to go," the ruddy-skinned guard said with a chuckle.

"Anyone else hungry?"

The guards doubled over with laughter before stopping to glare at the faces of the prisoners left in the room. I bowed my head with my shoulders slumped. He marched toward me as I stared downward at his blood-streaked boots. Bracing myself, I mentally prepared to be struck with the butt of a rifle.

"He's a quiet one. Let's start with him, shall we?"

After a brief gap of silence, a syringe jammed into my forearm. Within two seconds, my world faded to black.

An unknown amount of time had passed before I woke with a pounding headache and my vision splintered into fractals. Abstract images flashed in my conscious as I struggled to remember who and where I was. My fingers explored the searing sensation on my right cheek below my eye. My index finger outlined swollen bumps of skin, unbroken, and covered with transparent grease. The back of my neck burned, my fingers trailed over a thin bandage about an inch long. My eyes narrowed at the painfully bright space, sterile white and void of windows. I sat up on the stiff gurney and my memories flooded back in fragments. It would have been better if I had come down with amnesia. The door squealed as it swung open.

"So, you're up. Let's go," a ginger man sporting a lab jacket said as he held the door open.

"Where am I? What happened to me?"

"You are being processed to Dregs Island. What do you think happened to you, geez?"

I scrambled to stand, stumbling a few times due to the swaying floor. Fighting the disorientation from being unconscious, I moved into a long hallway lined with wooden doors, passing a loud whine of a motor within one of the rooms. As we passed, I glanced through a circular window at a horrific scene. I winced as one of the females who had previously been chained to a bench across from me shrieked in agony as a man in a white jacket sawed her wrist with a chainsaw. My eyes darted to my hands as I struggled to comprehend if I was perceiving reality or in a dream state. Either way, both of my hands were intact.

"We're going to the item room on the other side of the ship. You'll be able to select one survival tool from the wall. I hate to say this, but a boy like you won't even make it to the sand," he said with a laugh.

After traveling a few winding staircases and narrow passageways, we entered a slender room filled with stale air. Fishing poles, nets, and an assortment of knives and other weapons were fastened to the wall. I perused the choices of insect and other animal repellents, sunscreens, a flashlight, matches, rope, or a crude water filter. There was a wooden cabinet with glass windows. The cabinet was full of red glass vials marked with the word *cyanide*.

"If you want to end it without suffering," the white jacket man said with a one-shoulder shrug. "But that's the coward's way out. I've only seen two girls choose that one."

"I can select one item from this wall? Where am I going? What is this island?"

"I don't know where you've been lately, but prisoners in the United States convicted of a felony are banished and transported immediately to a prison island. You are headed to Dregs."

"Why is it called Dregs?"

He laughed and shook his head.

"Never heard that before? It means scum, refuse. You're being thrown out like an old banana peel."

"But the judge never told me how long I'm supposed to serve?"

"All prison sentences are for life. No matter what you did - rape, assault, murder, or even cat burglary. They don't fund prisons anymore. You had a trial and were found not to be fit for the Neoteric Society of America - President Gray's new social order as he named it years ago."

"I vaguely remember hearing about some type of new society when I was a kid, but never realized it was like this. Never cared since it didn't affect me," I said, as my eyes scanned the items on the wall.

"Hey, you've got to choose something. The next guy's due in two minutes," he said with a sigh. "I can call time, and you'll get nothing."

"I'll take the fishing pole."

The ginger man shook his head with a smirk as he stood on a step stool to retrieve an industrial-sized fishing pole.

"The young guys always go for the pole. You think you'll have time to fish?"

The man cackled as he handed me the fishing rig. A quick squeak followed by a crash caused me to jump as the item room door swung open, slamming against the wall. We both swished around with fear on our faces.

"He's trying to escape," a gap-toothed blond woman in a white jacket said from the hallway.

The ginger man shoved me aside as a prisoner, bleeding profusely from both earlobes, sprinted into the room and lunged for an axe on the wall.

"Make the call," the ginger man said to the woman.

He shoved me out of the room and locked the prisoner inside with external deadbolts, as the axe sliced into the wooden door from the inside.

"We have a 3490 on Spar Deck two, item room four. Prisoner five," she said into her two-way radio.

I took giant steps backward, keeping my hand on the fishing pole. The axe collided with the door a few more times. The two white coats stood motionless without saying a word as if they'd experienced this scenario before. I peered over the side of the boat into the open blue waters. Thoughts of jumping flashed in my mind. I'd have never survived the jump, as the ship was enormous.

"On scene, Guard 739." A soldier with a goatee in blue camouflage stormed toward the item room door.

"On scene, Guard 1200." A soldier with piercing eyes raced in behind him, his assault rifle perched on his shoulder, finger tapping against the trigger in angst.

The ginger white coat gestured for me to stand back against the rail as he took an adjacent spot, the gap-toothed white coat remaining in place. She obviously didn't want to miss a thing. Five more guards arrived, all dropping to one knee with rifles perched on their shoulder.

"Ready," Guard 739 said, as he unlocked the first deadbolt.

"Ready," Guard 1200 said, as he took a knee and aimed the rifle at the entrance of the room.

Guard 739 twisted the last deadbolt, grabbed the handle and opened the door with a swift motion. The inmate was struggling to remove the axe blade from the wood of the door as the rifles blasted a barrage of bullets into his flesh. Prisoner Five screamed as his body jerked wildly, blood spurting, coating the walls, his limbs dancing in the smoke-filled air.

"Exterminated," Guard 1200 said, standing up.

The guards filed into a single line and marched down the hallway without a word. The female white coat grabbed her two-way radio. Smoke cleared around the bullet-ridden body on the floor, and the axe loosened from the door and landed on his back.

"Prisoner Five needs a body bag, Spar Deck two, item room four."

"Junkies, I swear," the ginger man said, shaking his head.

"I'm off to lunch early," the gap-toothed blond said with a giggle, as she turned toward the hallway.

I exhaled, realizing I had been holding my breath. The ginger man instructed me to follow him. Hunger pains set in. I tried to recount the last time I had eaten anything. I couldn't remember, but I was dehydrated and dizzy as I trailed him to a guard station in the center of the ship.

"Prisoner One is ready for isolation."

"Thanks, Dr. Riggs."

A burly man in blue camouflage who reeked of peanut butter stood up from a desk and placed handcuffs on me. It was challenging to hold on to the giant fishing rig as he shoved me down a staircase toward a deck lined with doors along the walls.

"In there," he said, pointing to a black plaque embossed with *Number One*.

I opened the door with trembling fingers and cuffed wrists, dragging my fishing pole as I took steps inside of a wood-paneled room the size of a broom closet. There was a slot in the door for me to put my hands through. The guard removed my handcuffs and offered me a small bottle of water and what appeared to be a dehydrated peach.

"Get some sleep. You'll need it. Be there in a few hours."

Inside of the room, there was only a small wooden chair and a bucket. The officer had a kind face, so the next words flew from my tongue.

"May I ask you a question, sir?"

At an instant, I remembered what had happened to the last prisoner who had asked a question. I held my breath.

"Shoot."

I exhaled.

"Where am I going?"

The guard put his face directly outside of the slot in the door and waited until we locked into a stare. His kindhearted expression turned hollow.

"Hell on Earth."

5 THE TUNNEL

A guard slammed the butt of his rifle on the door handle and a crashing boom pulsed through my chamber. I awoke with a full body jolt. With weary eyes and seized lungs, I stumbled to my feet, steadying myself against the wall. Sunbeams streamed across the bilge, and it had risen at least ten degrees higher.

"Prisoner One, time to head to the tunnel," a voice sounded from the other side of the door.

The door lock twisted, and the handle shot downward. I grabbed my fishing pole and staggered to where I was told to go. After I was in place, Prisoner Seven was instructed to stand behind me. Out of the original eight inmates who boarded the ship, we were the only two left. The guys in the blue camouflage uniforms busied themselves docking the boat next to a large structure. I became curious, wanting to ask my fellow inmate about the island, so I turned around. When I caught a view of Prisoner Seven, I regretted my curiosity and disregarded my questions. His face bore a striking resemblance to Freddie Krueger from the *Nightmare on Elm Street* movies with bright red, mangled flesh and a seared eye – the other eye was missing an eyelid. He hadn't appeared that way when we were chained to the benches.

"Prisoner One, let's go. Prisoner Seven, wait until you are ordered to move," the officer said, as he pushed me on the shoulder with the tip of his rifle.

I followed him to a long ladder bridging the ship to a bridge's entrance. A thick, clear plastic tunnel spanned what appeared to be miles ahead. It reminded me of an over-sized version of the colorful tunnels in children's play yards. In the far distance, there was a landmass surrounded by towers. Dregs Island.

"In you go," the guard said, pushing me with a stern palm.

"What do I do?"

I took slow steps onto the ladder toward the plastic tunnel, dragging my fishing pole along my way. I regretted choosing the item and should have picked a knife.

"You'll figure it out," the guard said and slammed the ship's door shut.

The bright sun burned my eyes as I climbed down the steep ladder toward the tunnel, with sweat streaming down my back. After a near slip, I descended onto a wooden platform. A colorful sign spanned the archway of the plastic tube that said *Dregs Island. Point of No Return.* Seagulls sang in the sky as they swarmed on the other side of the ship. My feet stepped inside of the muggy passageway, my head brushing against the ceiling.

Gasping for breaths of oppressive air as I traveled the sweltering walkway, I avoided looking downward at the water below. I had two childhood fears - heights and the ocean. After making my way a stretch down the tube, I stopped to readjust my fishing pole and gather the courage to continue. Gazing through the plastic wall, I found the answer of why the birds were flocking on the other side of the boat. I recoiled with disgust as naked human carcasses floated in the water. The bodies danced within the splashing waves as they were consumed piece-by-piece by a school of skinny sharks with huge mouths. The seagulls swooped in from the sky, diving toward the water and then flying off with fins hanging from their pointed beaks.

"The six missing inmates," I mused.

Without a clue of what was in store for me at the end of the tube, I contemplated whether to continue toward Dregs or stay in the tunnel. Deprived of food or water, I was doomed. Prisoner Seven, who had chosen an axe and now resembled a monster, would join me at any moment. I hoisted the fishing pole onto my shoulder and pushed toward the island.

By the time I neared the end of the plastic cylinder, my knees ached, muscles were fatigued, and I had slowed to a crippled crawl. The thick jumpsuit was burdensome. I considered removing it but didn't want to expend the energy taking it off. The fishing pole's weight had more than tripled and I had switched to dragging it by the tip. I wanted to lie down and rest on the hard plastic floor, but the steamy air forced me to continue. Delusions flowed through my mind, of making it to the island and finding a lovely palm tree to nap under with a gentle breeze and ambiance of roaring ocean waves. Thoughts of paradise made it bearable.

My mother's face with reddened, teary eyes and swollen cheeks plagued my mind as I walked the last segment of the tunnel. I wondered what she and Tony were doing and how they were dealing with my absence at home and my banishment to the island. My father had abandoned her the night before Tony was born sixteen years before. I was an infant at the time, so I had no memories of him. She had worked three jobs to raise my brother and me. My heart ached for her.

It was still daylight when I reached the end of the tunnel.

"No way," I shouted as I shuddered at the water at least a hundred feet below.

Standing on the edge, I searched for a safe route to Dregs. The passageway had ended abruptly. No ladder, no slide. Nothing. Guard towers circled the island with one close on either side. There was no alternative to jumping into the ocean and making it to shore. I thought I might die upon contact with the ocean's surface, as I wasn't a skilled high diver and had never learned to swim. I studied the beach, realizing it would be a lengthy excursion to make it to sand after hitting the water. I had *doggie paddled,* as the girls called it while swimming at the recreation center as a kid. I had to rely on the method if I wanted to survive. Growing weaker by the minute, the base of my skull suddenly elevated in temperature at an unnatural rate underneath the bandage at the nape of my neck. My core heated up, and I became dizzy, befuddled. I slid my fishing pole beside me and sat down on the ledge, dangling my legs. I ripped off the bandage and raked my fingers across my neck. My skin felt like a warmed stovetop, and there was a raised ridge with a sharp scab. A linear splotch of burgundy blood had soaked into the bandage, but it was dried. Whatever was happening inside of my neck was abnormal. The tunnel had been unbearably warm, and my body was overheated, but something else had control of my physiology. The overwhelming heat radiated into my throat, constricting my breath. I forced a few swallows and struggled for air. Sweat streamed from my pores as my body succumbed to the warmth.

Desperate for the cooling effects of wind and water, I grabbed my fishing pole with both hands and threw my body off the tunnel's edge, my stomach filling with rocks. After a turbulent free-fall, my feet slammed against the water, jarring my neck. My body plunged into the abyss like a bullet from a gun. Throbbing with pain from the brunt force of impact, my skin soothed from the cool water. As I lost momentum, I heaved my arms to the side, struggling to hold my pole with my fingertips. Completely engulfed in the murky water, I tried not to panic as I searched for sunlight with one eye open. The deep water was disorienting and filled with dark shadows.

Stupefied, I struggled to swim, hoping I had chosen the right direction toward the surface, as my lungs only held enough oxygen for one chance.

After a few strokes, something struck my side and drove me through the water with enough strength to catapult me upward and into the air. I had flown for a few feet before I dropped back into the ocean. *What the hell was that?* My heart pounded. I fought to keep hold of my fishing pole as my head popped out of the water. With my tired legs kicking furiously in every direction, I searched for the shore. Fatigued, a guard tower was closer, so I made my way to the bottom platform and climbed aboard. I didn't know what had hit me, but I had a good idea and the sense to get out of the water if I wanted to live. The waves thrashed against my body, draining the little amount of energy I had in reserve. I gained my footing and steadied myself with the fishing gear as I caught my breath.

"Prisoner One, you are trespassing on the private property of the United States of America. Remove yourself at once, or you will be incinerated," a speaker sounded.

I searched for the voice's owner in a panic. The tower to my right had three snipers, all with guns directed at me. The structure to my left had two snipers aiming their weapons in my direction. Directly above, a guard in blue camouflage pointed a machine gun barrel at the top of my skull.

"You win," I shouted and hurled myself back into the water.

With every limb in action, I pushed myself toward

the beach – keeping my future nap under a palm tree at the forefront of my mind. Before I could make it to the sand, something rammed me in the stomach and knocked the wind out of my chest. My head went under water for a few seconds before I emerged topside. As I wheezed for air, my torso was slammed again and propelled away from the island. My energy was running dangerously low as I stabbed my pole blindly into the water to no avail. Gasping, I floated on my back while I inflated my lungs.

Once again, I paddled toward the shore for a few strokes until a pointed dorsal fin breached the surface in front of my nose. Two more fins followed behind it, and after a blink of an eye, fins moving around me in a synchronized manner circled me. They quickly created a swirling water current that made it harder to keep my head above water. Like a slide show, my mind revealed vivid images such as my mother sobbing in a black dress. My younger brother wiping a tear at my memorial service followed. Then, flashes of me at my fifth birthday party at the circus, waking up on Christmas morning when I was ten, and then of me walking the stage at high school graduation. *This is how it ends. They'll never know what happened to me.*

A voice rang out from the shore, and I swished around to see a man climbing into a makeshift canoe. With an arm threaded through a life preserver, he paddled toward me with vigorous strokes. Lifesaving devices had been among the choices in the item room of the ship. He tossed the float high in the air toward me, and it landed outside of the impending circle of doom.

"Grab it. I'll pull you in," he said.

There wasn't much time before the sharks made a move, so I drew in a huge breath and doggy paddled between the two smallest fins. Clutching the float with an elbow, the man yanked on the rope. I shrieked as jagged teeth pierced my prison-issued running shoe. Stabbing pains shot through my leg as I grabbed my fishing pole and lashed out at the shark repeatedly, shaking my leg free. I kicked off from its snout with my bare foot as my rescuer yanked me toward the canoe and pulled me aboard. With my chin resting on the edge of the boat as I gasped for air, the fins moved toward me.

"Watch out," the man said.

A shark rose from the water with an opened mouth full of razor sharp teeth. There was a large fishing hook looped through the flesh of his cheek. The beast gnashed his enameled daggers and rammed the canoe, barely missing my face as I dodged him. I scrambled to my feet and took a seat on the wooden plank of wood stretched across the vessel, inspecting my bare foot. It was only a superficial wound. I heaved for air as the shark gave up the fight and swam away.

"Larry Bateman at your service," a slim man with dark bushy hair said as he tidied the rope of his life preserver and placed it inside the bow of the vessel. His limbs were covered in black hair, and he had an overgrown goatee. "Ah, the bastard stole your shoe, huh? Sucks! At least you still have your fishing rig.

Good choice, by the way." He extended his bronzed hand to shake mine as another shark struck the side of the boat, nearly capsizing us. "Whoa, these guys are angry, huh?"

I slid into the middle of the seat, and he dredged his paddle in the water to angle the canoe in the correct direction.

"I'm Alex Cardin. Thanks for rescuing me."

"Ah, don't think anything of it. Just saw you struggling out there, and thought I'd lend a hand."

Larry rowed toward the shore as I looked out for sharks. Other than the guard towers surrounding the island, it appeared as paradise, a vision I'd seen before on a vacation pamphlet.

"Um, yeah, well, do many make it to the beach?" I said.

"About fifty-fifty, I'd say. That's why there are so many sharks over here. They circle the island and wait for their next meal. Easy pickins. But murderers are strong and always seem to find their way to shore."

"Murderers?"

"Yeah, like you. Your kind's stronger than most. Must be some reason for it," he said with a laugh. "Maybe because you guys suck the life force out of your victims, so you have supernatural strength."

He underwent a fit of laughter. *Why would he assume I'm a murderer?*

"But, I'm not a murderer."

"Ah, sure. Well, don't mention that again, young chap. Not on Dregs Island."

The boat approached a large mass bobbing in the

water. It was covered by a torn prison-issued jumpsuit. As we glided by, I shuddered at the sight of a disemboweled human torso with the intestines swimming in the waves like jellyfish tentacles. Without warning, the body disappeared, yanked downward into the deep.

Larry paddled to the shore, and the water calmed over the next five minutes in the hot sun. My adrenaline settled, and the reality of my situation hit me. In a new world without rules, I was far too naive to survive. My brain hadn't had time to process or plan. I had no strategy, no experience on the streets. I was doomed. As we approached the sand, I mused about how I would die. *Will it be quick and painless, or will I suffer?* The boat arrived on shore and Larry hopped out of the canoe. I jumped out and helped him move the craft to a safe place between two large palm trees.

"Where'd you get your clothes? I see you're not burdened with one of these heavy suits."

Larry donned a pair of green shorts with a beige button-up shirt. His clothes were handmade, but much more comfortable than my rigid suit that had gained over ten pounds of water. Furthermore, with snipers pointing their weapons from the towers, I didn't feel safe wearing neon orange.

"Oh, I'll hook you up, don't worry. There's a guy in Purgatory who makes rad garments out of silkworm thread. Used to be his job back on the mainland. He's been searching for a new fishing pole. He'll make the trade."

"That'd be awesome. I hope he has shoes, too."

"For sure."

We set off in the sand. Upon touch, the nape of my neck had cooled to the norm. I no longer felt like I'd swallowed a ball of fire. I convinced myself the incident on the tunnel's ledge was due to exhaustion with a possible twist of delirium.

"So, does everybody get along here? I mean, isn't this where our government sends felons?"

I followed Larry's lead along the beach. Missing a shoe, I walked with a slight limp dragging my fishing pole in the hot sand.

"For the most part, we've formed somewhat of a society. There are good folks like us and some not-so-good people. I'll show you the ropes. You can live a good life out here. It's not as bad as people on the mainland try to make it out to be."

I halted in my steps as voices screamed from behind.

"Ignore them, keep going," Larry said.

I allowed curiosity to plague my tired mind and I turned around.

"Stop right there," a man carrying a fishing pole with a broken line shrieked as he stormed toward me. "You're gonna pay for what you've done!"

6 PURGATORY

I buried my feet in the hot sand. Larry took a few steps back, begging me with his squinty eyes to avoid confrontation.

"You made me lose my fish, so go fetch me one, or I'll light you up," a scarred man in a filthy prison suit said as he pointed a serrated knife at me.

The man tore off a grimy ball cap, throwing it down on the sand and revealing a mangled mess of dirty blond hair. The hat had left an uncomfortable looking indention on his forehead. A short bald man with a broad face and rounded belly planted his feet to his left. He scowled at me with crossed arms.

"I'm confused. What'd I do?"

"I had a big'n on the line, and you made it escape. Now, you go catch one, or I'll be forced to hurt you real bad. Took all day to snag that bite."

I gazed at Larry with a mystified expression, but he countered with a blank stare. The angry man was just short of growling at me like a wild animal as he waited for me to respond.

"So, you're blaming me for your fish getting away? Because I dropped out of the tube and made my way to the beach? Doesn't that happen often?"

The bald henchman took a step toward me and kicked me in the shin. I stumbled backward, my leg throbbed until a blast of adrenaline eased the pain.

"What the hell? What was that for?"

Wanting to retaliate, I balanced myself and decided to stay civil.

"You don't talk to Dirty Pete like that. You made him lose his hook, and you gotta pay," he said in an unnaturally high voice.

Dirty Pete grabbed me. His arm was covered in mottled, shiny red ridges and valleys. He squeezed, digging grimy fingernails into my shoulder, sending surges of needle-like tremors down my arm. He slid the knife under my chin, the cool blade against my throat, slicing my flesh with a delicate burn. His breath reeked of rotten fish as he spoke.

"I'll say it one more time, kid. You've an hour to catch me a new fish, or you'll regret your first step on shore."

His sinister blue eyes glowered at me in silence, putrid breath assaulting my cheek. The blade sunk deeper into my neck, the stinging sensation intensified as a few drops of blood tickled my skin. Larry sighed, moving toward me.

"Hey, hey, hey, there's no need for this."

Larry poked Dirty Pete in the shoulder, and after a long second, he released the knife from my throat as his hairless minion stepped closer to Larry, panting like a vicious dog waiting for an attack command. I wiped the blood from my neck.

Dirty Pete released his vice grip on me as he and

Larry locked into a stare, sizing each other up as they planned their next moves.

"We don't want any trouble, man," Larry said. "But you'll have big trouble if you don't let young Alex go. Right now."

"Not scared of him. He's prob'ly an innocent."

Pete stared at my face with a menacing grin revealing yellowed, cracked teeth.

"No, not this one. You're mistaken."

Larry advanced toward him.

"But he made me lose my fish."

"I'm not joking, Pete. This guy's killed over twenty people in cold blood since he was twelve. There's no way he's innocent, he confessed to everything. Tobias will want him in leadership," Larry said with a powerful stare.

Dirty Pete lunged for me, pushing me backward into the burning sand. "For the record, kid, nobody scares me. Tell Tobias I said hello," Pete mumbled. He tapped his hairless underling on the back and shook his head with a foul grimace.

I climbed to my feet, brushing off the sand from my wet jumpsuit. After digging my pole out of the beach, I kept eyes on my newfound foes as they stormed away.

"Man, what was that all about? What'd I do to him?"

I rubbed my shin to ease the discomfort and then checked to see if my neck had stopped bleeding. There was no blood, only a stinging pain as I touched the area.

"I believe one of the sharks around you earlier was hooked on his line. He blames you."

"He's fishing for sharks?"

"That's all we can get here, Alex. Sharks taste pretty good."

"If it's what he does, then how hard could it be to catch another one, geez?"

Larry grinned and wiped the sweat from his brow. "Bait's difficult to come by on the shore."

I shook my head as something caught my eye at the shoreline. An abnormally large man in an orange jumpsuit washed up on the beach, crawling a few steps before standing.

"People swim to shore all day, right? I mean if all felons are sent here, I'd think there would be way more people here, no?"

"We're not the only island used as a prison. Other than that, the majority of felons don't make it here for various reasons. President Gray legalized accelerated capital punishment. You're lucky you dodged that one, as most murderers get that sentence and are killed right after losing the trial - that's why we have a limited number of killers on the island - albeit, we still have around five hundred or so. We have a legendary serial killer that lucked into the island instead of the needle. Others just never make it during the transport on that boat. We call that ship *The Bloody Executioner*."

I kept my eye on the naked man at the shoreline who was wringing out his wet jumpsuit.

"There were seven others transported with me, and

only two of us made it."

"I was the only one in my batch of fifty inmates that made it to shore. Darn brutal what happens to people on that ship."

"So what are the other reasons that people don't make it to the island?"

"Some turn into shark chum, some are blasted to bits or incinerated by the tower feds. Keeps the island population down. We'll have a serious problem one day with over-population. It'll be a dreadful situation, but the US government doesn't care one bit."

"Does anybody ever make it to shore from the tunnel bridge without help?"

"I'd say half never emerge from the water once they jump off. Either the jumpers die upon impact, or they turn into fish food. But a few saps make it by themselves - like that big lug over there."

The large man, now dressed, surveyed the beach with one hand shielding his eyes from the sun.

"You helped me get on the island, and I owe you one, Larry."

"No problem."

The human giant marched closer. I gasped in horror as I recognized the shaggy facial hair from the Texas jail cell. It was Joe. He was wearing war paint on his cheek and holding a machete. If I wanted to survive on this patch of malevolent paradise, I had to keep out of his sight. My brief communication with Joe back in the holding cell was all I needed to know the man wasn't wired right. He had openly admitted to murder, and the war paint on his cheek confirmed my fear that he was deranged.

"Let's go. Now, please."

My feet took me on a brisk walk without a clue where to go, so after a few steps, I halted.

"You know that guy or something?"

"You can say that. I met him back in the holding cell, in Texas. He talks like a pirate and might be a pedophile or something." Joe drew closer, and my heart clobbered the inside of my chest. "Something isn't right about him."

I shuttled around to the other side of Larry.

"He's no pedophile, Alex. He's a murderer."

"Yes, he was proud of that fact. But how did you know that? Because he chose a machete as his item?"

Larry sensed my urgency, and we picked up the pace to increase the distance. My nerves made me disregard my unanswered question.

"Yes, I suppose so, Alex. Let's head to Purgatory."

Purgatory?

Being in good physical shape, I didn't have a problem walking on the hot sand at first. But after a trek across the beach, my thighs fatigued and the bottom of my bare foot ached. The fishing pole became a nuisance as it dragged in the sand behind me. *Why didn't I choose a knife or sunscreen instead of this thing?*

After spotting a trail of deep paw impressions along the shore, I cleared my throat to get Larry's attention.

"What kind of animals are on this beach?"

"Ah, there's an assortment, but no worries. I'll

show you as we go - we've got it all worked out. Just follow protocol."

We passed the trail of prints and forked off in the opposite direction down the beach. Glancing over my shoulder, I kept an eye on Joe as he cut in toward the island, no longer following us.

"I'm so hungry." The words rolled off my tongue. The dried peach on the boat was the last piece of food I had eaten in over twenty-four hours. "How much further, Larry?"

"Ah, Mark's just around these trees. Let's score your threads and then get some grub," he said.

The final uphill stretch to our destination was the most painful. The top of my naked foot stung from the shark's graze, the sole tender from burning sand. My shin throbbed, and I was depleted of energy stores. I couldn't have made it five more steps by the time we arrived at a large hut with a thatched roof. A tattered hammock was suspended in front of the house between two palm trees, and a line of handmade clothes draped over a line with dye dripping onto the sand below.

"Mark, you in there? Brought you a customer."

Larry knocked on the door of the hut and then pointed to the clothes on the line and nodded. There were a few button-down shirts and shorts - all in different shades of pink and green, obtained from natural dyes of the plants of the island.

A demure Asian man shuttled to the porch holding a halved coconut in his hand.

"What can I do for you today?"

With a petite build, he was about a foot shorter than I was. He wore glasses and his straight black hair framed his rounded face. I found it peculiar he was missing his earlobes like Prisoner Five back on the ship, albeit this man's ears had healed. I wondered if it was some form of research the white coats were doing on the ship. I checked my ears - both were intact. I surveyed Larry's, and both of his earlobes were missing. My soaked one-piece suit had rubbed raw spots on my neck, legs, and back, so I decided not to bring up the topic. I needed something else to wear, no matter the price. I would have been happy with a palm leaf tied with jute.

"Do you have anything to fit me? Shorts, shirt, maybe some shoes?"

"Yes, I can help. But what do you have for me?"

Mark froze, feet planted on his porch of bound bamboo poles as he stared into my eyes.

Larry interjected, "He's willing to trade his fishing pole. You spoke about wanting one the other day."

He cocked his head, studying my pole with his narrow, dark eyes.

"Yes, the trade is favorable."

Mark swished around and disappeared into his hut for a few minutes. A familiar voice rang out from the other side of the trees surrounding the hut. Joe was asking someone where to find food and clothes. I glanced at Larry in a panic as he nodded for me to move a few steps where a tree would block Joe's view of me if he approached.

"Here you go. Shorts, shirt, shoes," Mark said as he

handed me the items and snatched my fishing pole.

Larry nodded for me to accept the items.

"Go ahead and change, Alex."

Mark held up his small, thin hand.

"Wait. May I have your suit and shoe? That is if you don't want them."

"Yeah, sure."

After an awkward pause, I jumped out of my jumpsuit, Mark accepted my discards, and I put on my new garments. The lightweight, dry clothes felt amazing - even though they were ill fitted. We thanked Mark and brushed off to find food just as Joe's booming voice and dimwitted dialect drew near Mark's hut. We had missed him by seconds.

"Close call," I said.

"It's a big island, Alex. Plenty of places to hide from that guy."

I struggled to catch my breath as I buttoned the last irregular wooden button of the green silk shirt. My new shoes weren't too bad - they were made of soft leather and stitched with a shiny material. They felt like a glove, soothing the burned sole and laceration on my right foot. Larry and I made our way to another hut down the shore where two guys were selling meat in a jerky form. I was starving, so I didn't inquire about the source. No matter what it was - I was going to eat it. Larry handed the man ten hand-rolled cigarettes in exchange for two bundles of palm fronds. He explained that cigarettes were the gold of the island, and smoking was considered a great luxury. There was one section of the island that grew tobacco plants, and it was well protected. I had tried smoking once at a party in tenth grade and nearly choked to death – or so I thought at the time. I didn't plan to start smoking, so I was lucky.

He passed me a palm frond as we ambled along the beach. I grabbed a piece of the jerky and took a huge bite. The meat was tough with a strong metallic, gamey flavor. At home, I would have gagged and possibly vomited. Nevertheless, it was nourishment, my stomach accepted it, and that was all that mattered. I'd have eaten rotten maggots covered with curdled cream if someone had offered.

"We will find a place to camp at dusk. We'll have to secure the area before we sleep. Too bad we don't have a residence here."

"You mean a residence, like one of the huts?"

"The huts in Purgatory are in shambles compared to other structures on the island, but yeah, they're better than sleeping out in the elements."

"How do you get one of the huts?"

"See, you don't want to stay in Purgatory, but if you must live here, you just figure out how to build one, or you claim one from the dead."

From the dead? I shuddered at the thought.

"That's why some structures here are real rickety. These people don't know what they're doing. I am taking you to The Quay – they are ultimately in control of Dregs Island. That's where the tobacco plants are, and there are cabins there – nice ones with fireplaces."

"Is that why that man on the beach told you to tell

Tobias hello? Does Tobias rule this place? Is he in The Quay?"

Larry hesitated.

"He's in The Quay, and he's in charge."

He paused to examine a group of palm trees.

"Did you mean what you said when you said he'd want me for leadership?"

"Alex, I was just saving your life. You learn to say whatever is necessary to survive. I know Tobias will take you in, though. Over there," he pointed toward two large palms. "We'll sleep here tonight and then head out at dawn. We can make it to The Quay in less than a day if we start early. You don't want to travel the Hub at dark."

"The Hub?"

"The center part of the island - it's the highest and full of trees, like a forest."

"What happens at dark?"

"It's just not safe at night. For that matter, never travel at night on the island - period. You're asking for trouble. You pick a place before dusk, secure it, and stick with it. Check for storm clouds, as well. Be quick and make a friend so you can stay in a residence if a storm comes, but you'll not need to worry about that once we make it to The Quay. I'm taking you there, so don't worry."

After a moment of over-analyzing his words, I gave up. I had no choice but to trust this man.

"Got it."

At the base of a palm tree, Larry dug a hole with his hands that was shaped like a shallow grave.

Following his lead, I did the same. Once deep enough, I climbed in, covered my legs, and built a pillow for my head. Larry sprinkled fluid with a pungent urine aroma around our burrows, and we polished off the packs of jerky. My eyelids grew heavy, and the moon was high in the cloudless sky.

"Me's glad me found a fren," a loud voice thundered.

I held my breath, turning my face in the opposing direction. It was Joe. A male voice responded, but I couldn't make out the words.

"Ye gots a house? A bed fer me?" Joe said, drawing closer.

Joe must have noticed us lying by the trees as he passed by only steps away. I strained my face toward the ocean, my neck burning from holding the position. My body shook so badly, I was half-afraid he would hear my muscles contracting.

"Yep, Joe. Right over there in that big hut," the voice said.

I lay still as Joe and the man went inside of the hut about thirty feet from where we chose to camp for the night.

7 MILA'S GROVE

"Time to get up, sunshine."

This was a voice from above, a few feet away - an actual voice, not one from my dream. Bewildered, I sorted out fantasy from reality. Sunbeams seared my retinas as I pried my eyelids open. The side of my face was caked with sand.

"Get up, so I can teach you a hard lesson of what it's like to be on the back end of revenge."

Larry stirred in his sandy cocoon. A foul stench invaded my nostrils as Dirty Pete leaned down within an inch from my face.

"Uh, Pete? I'm not sure what the problem is," I said, trying to free my legs from the sand. "Um, I thought you and Larry had worked this out yesterday, right?"

I blinked my eyes to focus, gulping at the sight of Pete's face. His left eye was gone. There was only a gruesome, blood-filled socket with orbit matter congealing on his cheek. The bloody cavity was something I had only seen in nightmares and horror flicks. His lips were white with fury.

"Wanna see what you've caused, killer?"

He shoved a bleeding stump of an arm in front of

my eyes. Along with an eye, a hand had also been removed. My eyes slammed shut, and I moved my chin against my shoulder. I was at a loss for words.

"They took my hand, and my eye, 'cause I didn't deliver a catch yesterday. This's your fault. They take from me, and now I take from you - I don't care who you are or who wants you."

I had hoped my only friend would mediate once again, but his shallow grave had emptied with a fresh trail of footprints curving around the palm tree.

"Larry?" I shouted as Dirty Pete yanked me by the shoulders and dragged me onto the beach.

He shoved me down, my bones bearing the brunt of the impact as my lungs lost their breath. I heaved to inflate them as he climbed on top of me. Blood trickled from the crater in his face and landed on my lip.

"First, I'll scoop out both of your eyes with this," he said, as he shoved a bloody ice cream scooper on top of the bridge of my nose.

There had been a metal scooper on the wall back on the transport ship. Someone along the way had chosen it as their one item. Purely pathological.

"Help!"

I turned my head in every direction. Larry had abandoned me. I was alone. Dirty Pete rubbed his bloody stump of a wrist against the side of my face with a maniacal laugh. It was warm, slimy, and had a stench of copper. I fought to remain conscious.

"Larry? You think *Larry* can save you now?"

"Wait," a feminine voice echoed from behind the

palm trees. "Pete, stop."

He twisted around and chuckled.

"Really? Mila, you think you can stop me? I've told you a thousand times that my name's *Dirty* Pete."

A young girl attired in a leather vest and cargo shorts marched toward us. She had an oval, beautiful face, bobbed blond hair, and an athletic build. I never would have guessed someone like her would be on the island.

"Not trying to stop you, Pete. I'll make you a deal."

"Deal?"

Dirty Pete sprang from his crouched position with a stern kick to my side. I struggled for my next breath as I wiped the blood, goo, and sand from my face with a palm frond.

"I'll catch you two sharks today, free of charge. But only if you let him go."

"What's he to you? You know this loser?"

He kicked me in the thigh, covering me with sand. I was far too nervous to feel anything. The girl glanced at me, sizing me up for a moment.

"No, I don't know him. I know an innocent when I see one. He doesn't deserve this. You need to leave him alone."

Pete laughed.

"You're not with The Compound anymore. Why should I listen to you?"

The Compound? I thought the governing part of the island was The Quay? This girl was unlike any other I had come across in my seventeen years. She was young, but spoke with the confidence of a seasoned politician.

"Pete, I've put a deal on the table. Two sharks by 4 PM. You can take the day off and nurse your wounds, but this guy goes free. Take it up with Tobias, not this poor fellow."

Dirty Pete sighed. After a moment, he stormed off. "3 PM or he loses both eyes and both hands."

Rolling my shoulder joints to ensure they were back in place, I thanked the girl. Compared to Larry, she seemed far more trustworthy.

"No problem. I can't stand it when they pick on innocents."

She held out a hand and pulled me to my feet. I was a head taller than her.

"How do you know I'm innocent?"

"You're not a killer. You've probably never committed a crime in your life. I've been on Dregs for three years. I've seen them come and go. I have a sixth sense about these things."

"Go? People get off the island?"

"No, they become shark food," she smiled, revealing the lone dimple in her cheek.

"Is there any possibility of escaping?"

"Don't even waste your neuron strength thinking about it. There's absolutely no way off. Many have tried, all have failed. Hungry?"

"Starving," I said with a smile.

The pain in my side and leg pulsed as we walked further down the beach into a more secluded area surrounded by what she called Evil Queen Trees. For a moment, I believed she was taking me somewhere private to kill me. She warned a single contact with a leaf would give a horrible rash and the fruit was lethal to consume. We made our way deeper into the brush, and she explained the steps to recognize a mango tree and how to retrieve the fruit. The branches overhead blocked most of the blistering sun within this space, but the thick vegetation prevented so much as a tiny wind gust from breaking through.

"Nobody realizes this fruit is here among the poison trees. It's my secret," she said with a laugh, as she picked a mango from an overhead branch.

"I'm Mila, by the way. And you are?"

She handed me some mangoes, and I placed them next to the tree.

"Alex Cardin. I'm from Texas."

"Me too, not that it matters anymore. I believe all Texas felons are sent here. There are rumors of more islands like ours, but who knows – it's not like we had a debriefing on that ship or anything."

She jumped down and exchanged her machete for a Swiss army knife from a handmade backpack. I was captivated by her sprightly manner. I was used to girls at school flirting and acting immature with nervous laughter. Mila may have been a few years older than me, but she was different. She displayed no interest in me other than an unemotional concern for my survival. This intrigued me.

"How'd they frame you?"

I leaned against a thick tree trunk as she prepared the fruit with her knife.

"I'm not entirely sure how or why I'm here. I

witnessed an accident. I reported the license plate of the car that hit an old woman, and here I am."

She shook her head with a sarcastic smirk and handed me a piece of sliced mango with a prosthetic hand. I hadn't noticed it before.

"What happened to your hand?"

I figured she would say whoever was making Dirty Pete catch sharks had done the same to her. She glanced at her false hand and shrugged a shoulder.

"I wished I didn't know anything about Dregs Island and that I could start over and just hide from it all."

She took a bite of mango and cocked her head, smiling.

"How did you know I was framed? How could you possibly know I was convicted of murder?"

"Alex, there's a ton you don't know. If I were you, I'd prefer to keep it that way, trust me. I'll tell you what to do to survive, and the rest is simply politics, negative thoughts to fill your mind. Your head will be stress-free if you stay out of it. I wished somebody had done that for me."

I finished my fruit with my mind whirling. I had too many questions.

"I saw huge animal prints along the beach. What lives on this island besides humans?"

"That's something you do need to know. The big problem here is tigers. They come out at dusk, hunt at night. There's an assortment of monkeys, birds, and of course, a huge amount of poisonous frogs, spiders, snakes."

"Ah, so Larry must've used tiger repellent last night around where we slept. I kind of recall seeing some various animal repellents on the ship in that item room."

"What was the guy's name who ditched you?"

"Larry Bateman. He saved me from the sharks and then from Dirty Pete, but then he disappeared this morning - right when I was about to have both of my eyes removed with a scoop. I thought he was a good guy, but— "

"I've heard a bit about him, but don't know him personally. Looks like he didn't have your best interest, huh? Took off when you needed him most. You shouldn't rely on anybody."

"I didn't imagine this place would have the most trustworthy people on it. I was just a fool to count on the first guy I met."

"Do you trust me?" she said with a half grin, slicing another mango.

"Not sure, to be honest."

She passed me another slice.

"Well, let me earn that trust. Come here, Alex."

She guided me through a narrow pathway with a hammock suspended between two poisonous tree trunks.

"Take a good, long nap. It's a bit muggy in here, but it's safe. You need it. I'm going to make good on my promise, so Pete leaves you alone."

"But— "

"Alex, you'll be okay. Nobody on Dregs knows about this place. Not even animals come through here.

I'll be back by 3:30 PM, I promise."

"How do you know the time? You don't have a watch."

"You learn the position of the sun over time." She smiled.

Begrudgingly, I climbed on the swinging bed of rope. I didn't have a choice but to trust her. It wasn't long before I drifted to sleep in the sultry heat.

"Wake up, Alex," Mila said.

With my nerves on guard, I woke at once, rolling off the hammock.

"Pete's all taken care of. However, I've got to go. I'll slice more fruit for you, but I won't be able to sleep here tonight. You'll be on your own, but you'll be fine."

I scrambled to my feet and followed her to the mango trees.

"What's Purgatory, The Compound, and The Quay?"

"Oh, just what people call parts of the island. People segregate. That's to be expected."

"Where are we now?"

Mila laughed, chunking mangoes to the ground.

"Mila's Grove. I told you, Alex, nobody knows this section of the island is habitable. On the other side of my secret place, there are tons of venomous snakes, and no one dares to go over there. My area's not very big, so don't venture out beyond the circle of poisonous trees and stay quiet."

"Why'd Dirty Pete lose a hand and eye for not

catching a shark?"

"That's Pete's responsibility. Everybody has a job on the island who wants to live as part of the overarching society. You've met Mark, I see. He makes clothes. There are various food merchants around Dregs - you can't survive forever on just mangos, so you'll have to buy from them. There are a couple of doctors - one's a surgeon - a very gifted one."

"Wow. If it's so civilized, why'd Pete get severely disfigured for not catching a shark?"

"I never said it was civilized, Alex."

We picked up the mangoes and walked back toward the hammock.

"Here, I'll just leave this with you, and you can cut your own," she handed me a small paring knife out of her backpack.

"What is your job, Mila?"

"Don't have one anymore, Alex. I'm kind of a fugitive among outlaws," she said. "I'll try to check back with you tomorrow if I can."

Without another word, she vanished. I was left alone once again. With no animals rustling the branches, no birds chirping from their nests or bugs buzzing, my mind unsettled as I sat in silence. It wasn't long before paranoia set in and plagued my brain. I convinced myself that even if the islanders didn't know the secret hideaway existed, they could find it just as she had done. Until the sun rose again, I laid in the hammock with my arms crossed in a protective stance, knife in hand. Visions of my mother and brother played in my mind repeatedly. I longed for the safe life I had left behind only two days before.

8 THE MARKS

Streams of sunlight crept in through the leaves, sprinkling onto my face. The night in Mila's Grove had been challenging - cold and alone with tigers roaring in the distance. I picked some fruit and waited for Mila to return, but by the time the temperature had reached its highest peak, I figured she had left me there without plans of returning. She had warned me not to trust anyone. My cynicism intensified, and I created theories of her keeping me there for an ultimate sacrifice, or maybe to use as tiger or shark bait. With a belly full of mangoes and in desperate need of interaction, I made a dreadful mistake when I left the confines of the secret sanctuary.

Noticing Mila had wiped away the tracks leading to the hideaway, I grabbed a palm frond and trailed it behind me, erasing my footprints. As I neared Mark's hut, Joe's voice thundered. With quick steps, I pushed my venture further into the island.

Deeper into the village, I came across many types of structures made of thick tree branches or bamboo poles bound together. It resembled a primitive settlement in an underdeveloped country. The heat of the day forced folks inside of their domiciles, but there were a few individuals outside boiling water, cooking, and making crafts. From behind small shrubs and huts scattered about, I could see faces of all kinds peeking out at me. Once they got a view of my face, they quickly looked away, avoiding interaction.

"It's mine, now give it back," a lady in a cutoff prison suit shrieked.

A man danced in front of her holding a coconut while pretending to be a monkey.

"I'll get my machete and take your head if you don't give it back," she said, gazing in my direction as she spoke. "Or, I'll get him to do it for me."

After a quick assessment, I realized these two were insane and acted irrationally. I took a brisk walk past them toward a large structure with cutout awnings propped up with sticks. Two heavily tattooed men burst out of the front door, growling, and shouting. I jumped to avoid them as they rolled on the ground, throwing punches and reaching for weapons. The larger one wore a military buzz cut and the other had a long ponytail striped with gray.

"Don't. Ever. Call. Me. Crazy. Again," the buzz cut man shouted, as he punched the man in the jaw with bloodied knuckles.

The underdog clambered towards me as the buzz cut man stood up. I stepped to the side, scanning the area to see if anybody else was going to intervene. The only other witnesses to the fight scampered inside of their huts.

The ponytail man choked for air. "I didn't say that."

The aggressor stormed inside the hut, and the victim moaned as he cradled his jaw. I was about to lean down to help the wounded guy when the buzz cut man returned with a broad axe. I took a few steps backward.

"Please, don't," the injured man said with his palms up.

The weapon raised in the air, and the blade dazzled in the bright sun. My naivety led me to believe he was only trying to scare his opponent, so I continued to watch. With great velocity, he slammed the blade down onto his rival's neck, a mist of crimson droplets coating the air as his victim's head rolled on the ground. I fought a gag reflex as I inspected my clothes - now stained with blood.

"I told you never to call me crazy again," he said, as he threw the axe on the ground.

He glared at me for a few seconds and marched back inside.

The next few moments are a blur, but I must have fled the scene. The next thing I remember was approaching a massive, fortified wall. It was professionally fabricated, like back on the mainland - a sharp contrast to the community of makeshift huts and cabins I had explored thus far. Thick, meticulous lettering was scrawled on a wooden sign with the words *The Compound.*

"Stop right there, pal."

I halted in my tracks, searching for the source of the voice. The barrel of a rifle poked out from a square cutout in the wall.

"Um, I'm just walking out here, not doing anything wrong."

"Come closer."

Nothing in my life had ever taught me that moving toward a gun was a good idea, but I complied with the request, nevertheless.

"Red Stripes aren't allowed near The Compound."

"Red Stripes?"

"I have the right to shoot you where you stand, as you are within our perimeter."

I put my trembling hands up, my legs turning to jelly.

"I have no idea what you're talking about. What have I done? Why would you want to kill me?" I remembered the blood on my clothes. "Oh, that's not from me. There was a guy back there. He cut someone's head off, and I had nothing to do with it."

I drew in a long breath, not knowing if I should run or try to reason with this guy. Mila came running from a distance with a palm in the air.

"Hold up, dude. He's an innocent, so back off."

She had flashed a stern expression at me before she approached the cutout.

"I'm innocent. I didn't do anything to get here. I was framed," I said.

"Alex, be quiet," she said. "Just let him go, I'll be responsible for him."

Mila walked toward the window.

"Alex," a familiar voice beckoned me.

I turned around. Larry Bateman stood behind me with a fresh gash on his cheek. He walked closer and placed his chin on my shoulder.

"Don't ever say that again, man. Not if you want to live another day. I have to get you to The Quay immediately."

"Where've you been? Why'd you leave me yesterday? I could've been killed if Mila didn't save me."

I turned to check on Mila, and she was engaged in a heated conversation with the gun-wielding guard. Larry tugged on my shirt to redirect my attention.

"You didn't see? They came to get me. When Pete showed up, some guys dragged me off, beat me up real bad - look at my face."

Mila finished her conversation with the wall sniper and joined us.

"I see your traitorous friend's back," she said with a sneer.

I shook my head. "It appears as though Larry was attacked as well," I said, pointing at his cheek.

"Good news, because I've important things to do today. May I have a quick word with you?" Mila escorted me a few steps out of Larry's earshot. She spoke quietly. "I told you to stay in the secret place, Alex. Do you have a death wish?"

"I'm sorry, Mila. I got paranoid, thought you were setting me up. I don't know who to trust. I apologize."

"Why do you have blood all over you?"

"Long story, but it wasn't my doing."

"Okay, don't tell your friend about my secret, alright?"

"You have my word."

"If you're not going to listen to me, I'm glad your babysitter's back. Stay out of trouble."

Mila took off toward the center of the island. My stomach filled with rocks as I regretted leaving her safe space. For some reason, I trusted her as if I had known her for years. I returned to Larry, examining the deep laceration on his cheek.

"Why'd they do that to your face?"

Larry dropped his eyes to the ground.

"Because I stood up for you. There's a lot that goes on here, Alex. The strong prevail, and, unfortunately, I'm not the strongest. Neither are you. For that reason, we must conform to the rules."

"Thanks, man. I appreciate you looking out for me."

"If anybody asks, the blood on your clothes is from your latest victim, and you're a serial killer thirsty for blood. Let's get to The Hub before dusk, shall we?"

I had a feeling that something wasn't right about Larry and his story about what had happened. Without a better option, I went along with his plan.

"Oh, okay. Ah, yes, the enchanted forest in the middle. Why do we need to go there?"

"It's the safest route to The Quay. You can go through the Battlefield to the left of The Hub, but that's more dangerous. You can go to the right of The Hub, but there are tons of lethal snakes, and nobody's stupid enough to go near that part of the island."

We had marched through the rest of what Larry referred to as Purgatory. Unlike the organized structure of The Compound, the houses were primitive with no protection around them. Larry explained that this section of the island was made up of individuals who didn't fit in any other division of Dregs. For all purposes, they were the rejects of the rejects.

"Did I mention that Purgatory's made up of mostly mentally ill people?"

"Yeah, that guy axed another guy's head because he called him crazy. I thought the insane went to mental institutions when they committed crimes?"

"Not anymore. Not since President Gray passed the prison reform bill."

"So, who are the people in The Compound?"

Larry halted his response as we walked by a group of five people in neon jumpsuits who were sitting in the sand, staring at us in an awkward silence.

"The Compound. Well, those are the smart folks. Doctors, lawyers, Wall Street types. They have all the engineers, scientists, lawmakers. When this place started six years ago, they grouped together and built that place to keep what they call *the undesirables* out."

"Shouldn't we join them? I mean, we're not murderers or rapists or anything."

"Alex, you're a Red Stripe. They'd never let you join their community."

"What's a Red Stripe?"

"Too bad there aren't mirrors here. You've been marked. They brand you during the transport to the island on the ship. Don't you remember it? You felt the needles in your face, right? That's how everybody here knows what everybody's in for – the mark. Kind of a sick joke by our government in a way."

As if a light bulb shined brightly above my head, it all clicked. I slid my fingers across my cheek, and it was still swollen and tender.

"Is it here?" I said while trailing the raised lines under my right eye.

"Yes, you have two red stripes tattooed on your face. You're marked as a murderer for life."

A vision of Joe's face flashed in my mind as he made his way onto the beach. I had thought it was war paint, but it was two red stripes under an eye. He had admitted to being a murderer back in the Texas prison.

"They gave me a shot to knock me out. I don't remember it at all."

"How humane of them," Larry said with a chuckle. "They've come a long way - they usually make you feel the pain. Somebody must have felt guilty and ordered you to be sedated."

"What are you here for?"

"I was a drug dealer. See, I've had my earlobes removed." He shrugged. "I sold drugs and got busted for it over ten years ago. They remove the earlobes for drug-related crimes."

"Pete's arm was burned. Is that a mark or did it happen here?"

"He's an arsonist, and that's the mark for arson - they set your arm on fire and burn ya pretty badly. He torched an apartment building in Dallas. He was angry with his girlfriend for cheating and wanted revenge. Lucky he didn't kill anybody."

We were yards away from The Hub's entrance with a grueling task in front of us to climb a large hill in the blistering sun. I needed stimulating conversation to distract me from the pain of the heat and physical strain.

"What other marks are here?"

"Have you seen an acid face yet?"

I evoked the terrifying vision of Prisoner Seven standing behind me on the ship.

"Yes. What did those guys do?"

"They're the worst, in my opinion. Pedophiles. Nobody has tolerance for them. If they're not killed by someone upon arrival, they're shunned to live in the Battlefield."

"The Battlefield?"

"It's a war zone and landfill between The Compound and The Quay. It's also where all human waste, island debris, and corpses are sent. Believe me when I say it's not a place you'd ever want to live. There are junk piles everywhere, and the smell is atrocious."

"So, The Compound fights with The Quay?"

"It's happened in the past, sure. The Quay bullies Purgatory, and The Compound stays out of it - they just take care of their own. Recently, Tobias has left The Compound alone for some reason - never been able to figure that one out." He shrugged his shoulders. "Have you seen a blue X on anyone's forehead?"

"What's that mean?"

"Rapists. They don't last long on the island, as

people are protective of their women. It's hard to come by true love here, and when it's found, they'll kill for it."

"My friend Mila had a missing hand. Is that a mark or maybe something that happened here?"

"She's a thief. If her dominant hand was removed, she participated in a violent crime, like a bank robbery with a weapon. If the other hand's gone, she's probably just a cat burglar."

"Mila has a prosthetic hand. Is that something you can get here on the island?"

"She probably has connections with the docs and engineers in The Compound. They are crafty and have all the knowledge on how to build stuff."

The steep hill was punishing as we climbed with the sun on our backs. Then, I thought of Pete and his punishment for not catching a shark.

"Pete had his hand amputated on the island, so I suppose you can't always go by the marks, huh?"

"Tobias may have considered Pete a thief, as he didn't deliver the sharks as promised. The eye removal was perhaps a show of authority, making an example out of Pete. Those in power will mark you if you commit crimes on the island. I believe the feds started marking us before our arrival to make the island divided, to cause segregation. Realize this - you've got the most sought after mark, so never claim innocence. People fear the Red Stripes, so use the gift to your advantage."

"But I'm not a murderer—"

"I've warned you - never say that again. In fact, say

you're a serial killer, and you'll be royalty."

I processed his words as we scaled the hot sand with slow steps, sweat droplets pouring off our bodies. He took a drink of water and then handed me a makeshift canteen.

"I'll play it by ear. Just not sure I can ever admit to being something I'm not."

"If you want to live, you will."

9 THE QUAY

Almost as comforting as walking into an air-conditioned store on a hot summer day, we took our first steps underneath the shade of the canopy. The chatter of monkeys and songbirds calmed me. Larry warned of venomous creatures lurking about, and I kept a watchful eye on the ground around my feet. He had explained The Compound stocked antidote for the toxins on Dregs, but never shared with marked people.

"How long of a hike is it to The Quay?"

"Ah, we'll get there by nightfall, no worries. Keep your eyes peeled, Alex. You can find treasures in The Hub from people who didn't make it the night before. Swords, fishing gear, backpacks of food, stuff like that."

"What do you mean by people who didn't make it?"

"People who try to travel The Hub at night. There's little chance of survival here at dark. The tigers on this island hunt at night and most live in The Hub. But the poisonous snakes, frogs, and hell, even some trees are darn near lethal. In the black of the night, you can hardly avoid any of it."

I slowed my steps as a white object came into view to the right of the footpath.

"Over there, what's that?"

I pointed at a plastic dome jetting out of the vegetation by a tree. A bright green snake hanging from a branch swung back and forth as if to guard it. Larry lunged over and snatched it, narrowly dodging the snake's swinging head. He leaped back onto the trail holding a helmet-like apparatus. The headpiece extended down around the neck, fastening in the front. Black rubber insulated the entire piece.

"Bizarre. What's that? Part of a stormtrooper costume?"

Larry surveyed me for a long moment in awkward silence before he spoke. "Whatever it is, we can probably get a few cigarettes in exchange for the raw materials. Let's take it with us."

"Okay, cool." I shrugged.

"Good eye, Alex. Keep up the good work," he said as he handed me the contraption to carry.

Something wasn't right. He had acted suspiciously as if he knew more about the item.

After a minute hike, I kicked a strange object in the middle of the trail. It was a large rusted ring holding five crude skeleton keys.

"I'll take those. Excellent raw materials - maybe we'll get a couple more cigarettes," he said, snatching it from my hand and sliding it into his back pocket.

"Do you think those keys open things on the island?"

"Not that I know of, but this place hasn't always

been inhabited by us prisoners. Remember, we've only been here six years. Others have used this island before, but I have no idea who, when, or why. I just know certain things that weren't available on the transport ship are here somehow. People have discussed theories over the years."

With only the crunching of leaves and buzzing of insects, we had made it to the top of The Hub. The sunlight faded under the thickened canopy, and the breeze had ceased to exist. I swore I heard tigers snoring, but fought to distract my mind. I didn't want the smell of fear to wake them.

As we trekked the decline down the backside of The Hub, my foot caught on a zigzagging branch that crossed the path. I tumbled a considerable distance before launching myself within a dense thicket of trees. My knee bone connected with something considerably hard on the ground underneath layers of underbrush. The pain kept me in a trance as I held my breath in shock.

"You alright?"

Larry jogged toward me.

"Yeah, just knocked my leg pretty hard on the ground right over there. There's something solid there, maybe metal."

Rising from a fetal position, I searched for toxic creatures while Larry felt around with his foot, moving the brush aside. I scrambled to my feet and pointed out the spot my knee had hit. We worked together to uncover a metal door with a recessed handle.

"Whoa, I've only heard stories of things like this being on the island. I didn't believe they existed," Larry said, slipping his hand around the handlebar and pulling with all his strength.

"What are you talking about - what kind of things have you heard about?"

He yanked on the door, the veins in his temples pulsated.

"Um, nothing really - just that uh, you know, like that weather shelters could be here."

I leaned over his shoulder and caught sight of a few wooden crates stacked in the bunker. The weathered boxes were stamped with red lettering, USMC with various series of numbers. Feigning to lose his grip, he released the handle, allowing the door to slam shut. It was evident he didn't want me to get a glimpse of what was inside, so I played along as if I hadn't seen anything and suspected nothing.

"Let's keep this a secret between us, Alex. Hush, hush. When lightning storms hit on this island, you need shelter. You can't be out and about, or you'll get fried - they've made sure of that. There wasn't much room down there, maybe only enough for only two people - you and me. If word gets out this place exists, we'll never get a spot, believe me."

"The shelter was empty?" I was testing his honesty.

"Nothing but a layer of dirt and cobwebs, but we'll be glad to have it if it starts storming while crossing The Hub." He moved the foliage back over the door and took a moment to survey the surroundings. "Let's go. That heavy door slamming may have woken the tigers. How's that knee?"

"It's sore, but I'll be fine."

A putrid stink resembling methane and hydrogen sulfide loomed ahead. After ten steps, we came upon a corpse on the side of the path. A man with two red stripes on his cheek. His skin was ghostly pale with a bluish green hue. Flies swarmed the decaying flesh, landing on his exposed wounds and dancing about as they hunted for a place to lay eggs. Lifeless, glazed eyes stared upward at the tree canopy, and four deep gashes spanned his neck, his torso covered in blood. The man was frozen in an awkward position against a tree trunk, clutching his weapon as ants and an assortment of beetles overran his body. Most of his abdomen and both legs were missing – one severed at the knee and the other at the hip. The stench overwhelmed me, and without warning, my stomach contents launched from my throat repeatedly. After about a minute, my lurches became futile. I stood upright with my hand on my belly to ease the cramping, trying to suck in air from my mouth to avoid the smell.

"Oh, man. Sorry. That's just, well - I've never experienced something that bad. The only dead person I've seen was freshly dead."

"No worries, it always happens the first time - you'll get used to it. Poor chap, looks like he met his fate with the big cats. He's a Red Stripe, should have known better than to be out here. Pry that machete out of his hand. Doesn't even have a drop of blood on it. He was taken by surprise."

With nothing left to throw up, I held my breath and sprung over to the corpse. With Superman's strength, I snatched the knife and took a brisk walk ahead on the trail.

"This dude must've been baking in the heat all day. Gross."

"Corpses also attract all kinds of creatures. You never want to be near them - especially if they're fresh. Freshly dead or even the injured act as tiger bait - tigers can smell the blood. They prefer the hunt, but the cats on Dregs will take an easy meal when they can. Not too far ahead, we're almost to The Quay."

"Speaking of bait, what do the fishermen use for shark bait?"

"We use all materials available on the island. You sure you want to know?"

"Yes, I do."

"Body parts. Chunks of torso preferred or maybe thigh meat. The sharks surrounding the island crave human flesh."

"People are killed for bait or do they use those who die on the island?"

"Folks die every day on this island, for numerous reasons. There's no shortage of bait."

A short distance in front of us, I spotted Mila crouching down in the tall weeds, making her way toward The Quay.

"Hey, there's Mila. I wonder what she's doing?"

Larry put his index finger on his lip, widening his wild eyes. "Be quiet. Let's follow her. Stay back and match her every move. Thieves are best at moving undetected, and I wouldn't mind learning a thing or two from her - especially if she's sneaking into The Quay."

We lurked in the shadows at the edge of The Hub and watched Mila snake through the tall weeds toward The Quay. She was far ahead, but never looked back at us. I didn't feel good about spying on her. I would have rather joined her, but I didn't want to cross Larry. A large chain-link barrier topped with barbed wire spanned the area. Two bulky men with yellow striped tattoos on their faces guarded the fence at the end of the trail from The Hub. They stared ahead with angry expressions, eyes scrunched, and each with a katana sword in their hands.

"What do the yellow stripes under their eye mean?" I whispered as we followed Mila's route behind a cluster of palm trees. "Those just faded red ones, or are they that color on purpose?"

"Assault. Closest to murder, so they're used as lookouts by The Quay. They're not real Junk Rats, though. They're wannabes."

"Junk Rats?"

We stopped behind wild bushes and watched Mila, as we'd be unable to track her while we crawled through the weeds. I wanted her to look our way so I could signal her without Larry knowing, but she never turned around.

"Those who live in The Quay. The Junk Rats report to Tobias."

"But why Junk Rats?"

"They don't call themselves that - just everybody

else on the island calls them that because they hate them. They are all murderers. They're ruthless. They rule Dregs."

"But The Compound's more organized with thick walls. They had rifles."

"True, but they aren't cold-blooded, and their ammo is limited. Tobias is well aware of this. They use those guns as a threat and aren't born killers - definitely don't have a propensity for violence. They'll only defend themselves when needed. Junk Rats, on the other hand, don't need weapons or reasons to kill someone. They spread pestilence and invoke fear."

"Why would I want to join them? I don't belong there. I'd rather join the nice guys."

Mila disappeared within the tall wild plants.

"I already told you, The Compound will never take you in - you're a Red Stripe, a murderer. They're only loyal to the no-marks - the white-collar folks. Never trust them, Alex, and there are no exceptions. You can trust Tobias - he always sticks up for his people. I've been trying to become a member of The Quay for years, but they don't trust *druggies,* as they call my kind. They often accuse us of being spies for The Compound. The best I can do is stay on their good side. I protect Tobias's people until they make it here to join him. Guys like you."

A stinging sensation surfaced on my leg as if I were being stabbed with a hot poker. I slapped at my leg, searching the ground for what had stung me.

"Ow."

"There he goes," he pointed at the ground, but I

couldn't see anything but grass. "Did you touch him?"

"There who goes? What the hell do you mean? Touch who?"

I panicked, investigating the ground.

"Don't worry about it. Once you become a member of The Quay, they'll get you an antidote from The Compound. Those darn banana frogs usually stay on tree branches. You see him over there?" He pointed to a bright yellow frog the size of a grape hopping away from us. "If you come in contact with his skin, you've got about 8 hours to live. Let's go. We're going to lose her. We need to crawl to that bunch of trees down there on the left, where she is right now."

8 hours to live? My heart pounded in my throat as I gasped for air.

"If you're on Tobias's good side, why can't we go to the front gate? I'd like to get the antidote as soon as possible."

"Like I said, I want to see how Mila sneaks in - just for my knowledge. You can learn a ton from thieves. You've got time, Alex. Trust me. Symptoms won't even kick in for at least an hour."

On our elbows, we dragged our bodies through the high grass to the left of the fence line. We followed Mila's depressed trail until we reached a mound of jagged rocks, and then we made a run for the trees. Mila was down past another patch of tall weeds, burrowing her way through a hole underneath the chain-link barrier.

"Is there any way to escape the island, Larry?"

The skin of my leg where the frog had contacted me had puffed up with bright red streaks forming around the bump. I drew in a calming breath, talking myself out of losing my mind.

"Not a chance, Alex. President Gray must've had a team of top minds think of everything when the island prison program was conceptualized. Your only chance of survival is serving Tobias. I wouldn't steer you wrong."

Mila shuffled into view on the other side of the fence. She was inside of The Quay, crawling on her belly toward a brick wall that traversed at least a half-mile toward the beach. After making it to the wall, she sprinted at top speed toward the shore. Lucky enough, she was just short of the wall in height and didn't need to crouch. We mimicked her actions with great caution, as there were many Junk Rats standing guard in various positions. I figured the wall was five foot tall, as I had to bend over considerably to move along the way without being seen. We caught up with her as she neared a shack-like building. I had a small heart attack as Larry screamed at the top of his lungs.

"Thief. There's a thief in The Quay!"

10 THE STORM

Mila spun around with her cheeks blushed and brows angled toward the bridge of her nose. She glared at Larry with her nose scrunched, eyes forming slits, and mouth gaped open. With a loss for words, I suspended animation.

"Thief! There's a thief in The Quay!"

I recovered my voice and shoved his chest to quiet him. "Larry, what the hell are you doing?"

He stumbled backward and then gained his footing.

"Thief. I found a thief! Over here!"

Like ants in a mound, Junk Rats materialized from all directions. As if on cue, the sky turned gray, and a soft rumbling of thunder boomed in the distance. My breathing became labored, and blood rushed to my face with the sting of betrayal. Larry grabbed Mila by the arm as she tried to escape. She struggled, but Larry was too strong.

"Larry, she's my friend. Why would you do this? Let her go."

Avoiding eye contact, he took steps backward as he released her, removing himself from the circle of Junk Rats that was forming.

"Go get Tobias," a woman with a narrow, oblong face wearing primitive battle gear shouted.

Within a few seconds, at least forty more Junk Rats surrounded us, shouting taunts. Larry vanished. Another sequence of thunder roared as grim clouds moved our way, darkening the sky as if someone slid a dimmer switch.

"I'm so sorry, Mila. I had no idea—"

"Just stop, Alex."

The circle thickened before parting ways to form a narrow walkway.

"Mila, please, listen to me—"

"Shut up."

From beyond the circle came the sound of organized footsteps. Mila glared at me, her body trembling with anger. Her jaws were clenched so tightly, her temples pulsated. A young boy with bleached blond hair marched down the passage and stepped up to us.

"Tobias, supreme ruler of The Quay, approaches."

The boy took a step to the side as a tall, dark, shirtless man wearing a burlap tiger tooth necklace strode toward us. He sported black dreadlocks to his shoulders and had a chiseled face with angular cheekbones and a pointed chin. Hieroglyphic tattoos surrounded his pronounced widow's peak. A loud thunderclap rumbled as he flexed his arms that both had full-sleeved tribal ink.

"Kneel in my presence."

Tobias had an air of power that was profound. Befuddled, my legs locked, and I thought my body was about to crumble. Mila dropped to her knees, and I allowed myself to do the same.

"I ask permission to speak," Larry said, ambling through the aisle.

The blond boy held up a palm, gesturing for him to halt at the edge of the circle's interior. Tobias didn't turn to face Larry. His dark, heavy-lidded eyes remained glued on Mila and me.

"Permission granted," Tobias said, his voice bottomless.

"I was transporting him here because he's an innocent with the mark – your mark. I know you don't want Quay imposters wandering around the island. The only Red Stripes on the island belong here, reporting to you."

My lungs constricted at his words. Larry was the worst kind of self-serving traitor. Tobias's eyes burned into my soul as I stood helpless, unable to defend myself.

"Accepted. And the female?"

"As we got to the front gate, I saw her sneaking through the tall grass around the side fence. I knew you'd want to know how thieves get in here to steal your supplies, so I followed her and reported it without delay. She sneaks in through a blind spot, a hole in the ground underneath the fence. I can show your sentries exactly what she did."

"I appreciate your loyalty to The Quay, but still do not grant your request for residency."

Larry hesitated, taking a moment to stare at the ground before he popped his head up.

"I'm just honored to serve you, Tobias. Also, I found a lightning helmet in The Hub," he pointed to the white plastic contraption I was holding, "and these keys - I believe they belong to The Compound. You could probably get something good in exchange for them."

The blond boy seized the helmet apparatus and machete from my hands. Larry handed Tobias the old set of keys. *Why was I so gullible?*

"One more thing, Tobias, if I may," Larry begged.

Tobias drew in a long breath of air as he glared in the distance. He exhaled as he turned around to deliver a scowl.

"Speak."

"In The Hub, there's a military bunker, fully stocked with grenades, guns, bombs."

Thunder rolled in the sky. I glanced at Mila who kept her eyes on the ground, shoulders hunched forward.

"If you speak the truth, you may serve The Quay as a sentry. Guide my people to the weaponry at once." He pointed toward us, "And someone take those two to the cages."

An earsplitting bolt of lightning struck the ground behind us. The hairs on my arms stood erect. I repeatedly blinked to refocus my eyes, for the brightness of the light had bleached my retinas. The thick electricity in the air was stifling as it filled my airways, but Tobias hadn't so much as flinched. The Red Stripes forming the circle cowered, all casting terrified looks at their leader.

"You five retrieve the weapons without delay," he shouted over the thunderous roar in the sky. "Take cover at once, Red Stripes of the Quay."

Larry rushed over toward a group of Tobias's followers. The circle disbanded and the Junk Rats scampered into the surrounding buildings. The blond minion and Tobias marched toward the largest building in the center of The Quay. It darkened even more as dense droplets trickled from the clouds.

A Junk Rat stepped toward us to escort us to a cage, and a bright flash of light appeared above his head. A booming noise sounding like a gunshot rang out, and his eyes rolled back into their sockets as his body convulsed. The lightning bolt flashed again, tossing his body into the air. The rest of the Junk Rats standing near us scampered into buildings.

"Run," Mila said with a frightened expression.

She swirled around and took off at full speed toward the wall. I trailed her every move, reversing the route we had taken to sneak inside of The Quay. The rain poured down in heavy sheets, making it difficult to crawl underneath the fence in the slippery mud. We sprinted at full speed up the tall grass hill toward The Hub. Covered in sludge, we laid flat against the ground as we watched Larry exit the front gate with four men in plastic helmet contraptions - one like I had found by the trail. They marched toward The Hub down the main trail.

"Larry's taking them to the bunker. He's such a traitor."

I punched at the ground and sent a painful

shockwave up my arm.

"Where is it?" Mila asked.

"Right after the top of the hill, when The Hub starts to angle towards The Quay, not too far off the trail on the right side."

"We must avoid them. They'll kill us and report we were trying to get to the bunker first. Those guys do anything to get on Tobias's good side. Stay off the trail and move through the trees. It'll be dangerous - keep your head on a swivel."

We waited a few minutes in the tall grass for Larry's group to move into The Hub. The downpour pummeled the blades around us and unveiled our hiding place. As if it were chasing us, another bolt of lightning struck in the field, and a high-pitched tone resonated in my ears, dizzying me and blurring my vision.

"We have to go, we have to find cover," Mila said and took off toward the forest of The Hub.

Following her lead, I chopped tree branches out of my way while jumping over logs and rocks, hoping not to stumble upon anything nefarious. The canopy blocked most of the downpour, but with the storm, it was dark as night. Agonizing spasms burned through my poisoned leg muscles. In a fight for survival, copious amounts of adrenaline and pure instinct kept my imminent death from the banana frog at the back of my subconscious.

"In here, now!" She dove for a gaping hole in a massive tree trunk - just big enough for us to crawl inside.

"If we stop, can we make it out of The Hub before dark?"

"Lightning will kill you, Alex."

"But what are the chances? I mean, it's not like we're metal or holding a lightning rod."

"The chances are extremely high. You've got a receiver in your neck, fused to a cervical vertebra. It attracts lightning - on purpose."

I raked the back of my neck where the bandage had been, detecting a small scar about an inch long.

"Receiver?"

Memories of the severe heat in my neck while standing on the tube's edge flowed into my conscious. My body temperature had soared without warning, forcing me to jump. It hadn't felt biological at the time. Now it made sense.

"Yes, Alex. They put a device on your cervical vertebra to control you, to track you, to kill you if they want. You're gone in a matter of seconds if they put in your code and send the signal."

"How do they do it?"

"They call it incineration. They signal the transmitter, and it cooks your body from inside. You'll die within about 2 minutes. I've seen people's eyes bleed before they collapse, it's gruesome. Good thing is, you have to either be in the water or at the shoreline - the signal doesn't reach beyond that."

"And the lightning?"

"I'm unsure if that was intentional or not, but the chips are electrical magnets. Wouldn't surprise me if it was on purpose - the United States government's so corrupt."

"What would you say the likelihood of lightning striking you is if you stood out in a storm?"

"99%. I've seen it many times. If you're out there, it finds you. That's why Tobias went for cover without delay. Wood, plastic, rubber - you've got to protect yourself with a non-conductive material, or you're toast. This tree is the safest thing for us - given our circumstances. We're not too safe, though. I've seen a bolt hit a tree that someone was hiding in before."

The storm gained strength as angry wind gusts swooped the tree branches over, hailstones clattered to the ground, and lightning flashed across the sky. Larry and his cohort disappeared into the bleakness of The Hub.

"I came into contact with a banana frog," I pointed to the rash that now spanned across my right leg. The pain was waning, but numbness was setting in.

"That's terrible. No one survives after touching one of those. One jumped on my best friend not too long ago."

My nervous system launched a nuclear attack on my conscious. I battled an acute panic attack as I choked out my next words. "There's nothing I can do?"

"From our arrival on this island, my friend and I worked for The Compound as foragers. We weren't officially one of them because we had marks," she flashed her prosthetic hand, "but since we were non-violent thieves, they employed us to gather things for them - even items from The Quay. In exchange, they kept us safe from the Junk Rats. The Compound's scientists make the antitoxin. They're the only ones smart enough to know how to make it. They use it and other drugs they make to get what they need from Tobias."

"Great. I have no leverage. I'm going to die."

I forced a palm onto my chest to steady my pounding heart and inhaled a bottomless breath.

"The Compound lost my loyalty the day they denied the request for my dying friend to get a dose of the antidote. I became desperate and broke into The Compound to try and steal some from the infirmary to save her life. They caught me, and I was banished. That's when I went rogue. Once I'm betrayed, I will never turn back."

"What happened to your friend?"

"She died, of course. And they didn't care."

I couldn't breathe as if someone was choking me. To retain my sanity, I entered a state of denial. It wasn't going to happen to me. I wasn't ready to die. We pushed further into the gap of the trunk as the unrelenting storm grew stronger, the wind whooshing anything without roots into the air. With an ear-shattering boom, a lightning bolt crashed against The Hub's trail about twenty yards from the tree. The chip in my neck vibrated, soaking up the surrounding energy. Everything sounded muffled in the distance as a persistent ringing noise twirled in my ears. Angst shrouded Mila's face as she jumped to her feet. Her demeanor abruptly changed.

"I got you this far, but because of what you did by

enabling that guy to blow my cover, we can never be friends again. By the way, the lightning's found us. You need to run."

She tore off down the footpath at full speed. Thunder boomed as blasts of wind bowed the trees, breaking off branches and carrying them toward the sky. I sprung out of the trunk just as a lightning bolt exploded inside of the tree trunk where we had just been huddled. The flash disoriented me, diminishing all of my senses. I couldn't tell which way to run, as the storm was all encumbering.

A muffled growl loomed behind me. I spun around to face a tiger, crouched on its haunches. It leered at me and dug its talons into the muddy ground, tensing, and snarling. At that moment, we were both making a decision. Avoiding eye contact, I bowed my head to search for anything to use for defense. Within a leap's distance was a huge rock. With a certain death from the beast or lightning, I lunged to grab the rock with both hands and threw it toward the cat's head like an Olympic discus thrower. Hoping to make it to The Compound, I shot through the forest, unsure if I had chosen the correct route. My irrational mind formed a plan to beg for shelter and the antidote. It was the only chance I had for survival.

After zigzagging through the dense forest, it seemed like miles before I burst out of the tree line and found myself at the top of a steep hill. Unsure if the tiger had even given chase, I never looked back. The side of The Hub was covered with jagged rocks and vertical gradients - a certain death to a climber who slipped. As I navigated down the sheer gradient, the formidable sheets of rain thrashed my back. My will to live kept me from tumbling down the hill as I stepped carefully on each rock's ledge and descended to the level ground. I started to recognize where I was, even with the blinding storm.

I caught sight of The Compound right before a bright flash of light consumed me like an alien abduction. Confusion swept in, overpowering me as every muscle in my body contracted, limbs turning rigid. A crushing, searing pain radiated through my body like a velociraptor was set free inside of me. I sailed into the air with every cell screaming for mercy. A burning sensation flamed at the base of my skull and then, everything went black.

11 THE COMPOUND

Distant noises brought me back to my senses. The throbbing in the back of my neck incapacitated me, and I struggled with tightened lungs. Every few seconds, the blackness returned as if someone was using a remote control to alter my existence.

"We don't save Red Stripes."

If nothing else, the words were clear. I forced my eyelids apart and managed to form a narrow slit in one eye. My vision was far too blurred. Everything appeared as a mosaic watercolor painting.

"Would you rather throw him to the sharks? I saw him the other day. He's an innocent. Mila spoke for him."

Blackness followed.

Time had passed before I awoke on a steel table. My head prickled strangely. A swinging ceiling light swam into view a few feet above my face. I swallowed a hard gulp and darted my eyes around the room.

"Where am I?" I mumbled while wincing at the blinding pain at the base of my skull. My sight had returned, albeit with halos around lights.

"Relax. You're in The Compound, Alex," a lady's

voice said.

I pushed up on my elbows. Stinging electrical pulses radiated from my cervical vertebra and exploded like a bomb in my brain. I dropped down, flat on the table. I tried to remember what had happened, but it made my head hurt.

"Alex, I'm going to give you something to make you feel better. You'll fall back asleep in a few seconds."

She stuck my arm with a needle. I recalled the banana frog and the toxins flooding through my body. I tried to get the words out, but blackness returned.

After an unknown period, I awoke once again to muffled sounds.

"Alex? How do you feel now? Your neck's been treated the best we can," a lady's voice said.

My eyes focused on her face - a smidge past middle age with a round face framed by jagged caramel hair. She was probably a beauty in her youth back on the mainland.

"Um." I surveyed myself. The only detectable pain was in my leg. It was a numbing ache - a throbbing that squeezed my muscles and constricted blood flow. "I came into contact with a banana—"

"Yes, I know. I gave you a dose of antitoxin. I saw the rash - know it all too well. Can you sit up?"

Before attempting to rise, I concentrated on my neck. It was sore, but not as unbearable as before.

"How long have I been here? Days?"

She laughed. "Alex, you've only been here a few

hours. The storm's over. Dusk is about to set in. Dr. Volkmann has approved a one-night stay. You are the first Red Stripe he's ever allowed inside of The Compound, you know. He also approved a dose of antitoxin for you - and that's another first."

My core muscles pulled me upright as to avoid straining on my neck. The room was small but clean. Medical supplies were arranged meticulously on a table made of bamboo poles. My clothes were neatly folded on a chair, and I was naked underneath a silk sheet.

"Dr. Volkmann?"

"Yes, he runs The Compound. He was a scientist back on the mainland, got nabbed for tax evasion, but he claims it was his accountant's fault," she chuckled.

"Who are you, and why are you here?"

"My apologies, Alex. I introduced myself to you earlier, but you must have been loopy from the medication. My name's Natalie Rose. I'm a nurse. I was sent to Dregs Island because I ran a charity and was paid from the profits. Found out during my trial that part of President Gray's reform outlined that nobody could earn wages from a charitable organization - even if they made it their full-time job. That's what I get for not keeping up with changes in laws."

"What kind of charity did you run?" I said, adjusting my sheet.

"I provided free medical aid for low-income neighborhoods. I quit my job in the emergency room to start the group because I was tired of having to turn sick patients away because of money. Funny thing is I made less than half my hospital wages to help people."

"You weren't allowed to be paid from your charity? That seems harsh. Who can afford to run such a thing?"

"My point, Alex. Nevertheless, here we all are." She sighed. "I hate to see those red stripes on your face. I knew you were innocent the moment I saw you. You're probably my son's age, you know."

"Really? You have a son? When did you see him last?"

"Five years ago. He was twelve."

"How's he doing now?"

"Oh, Alex. We can't communicate with the mainland," she said with a bowed head. After a long pause, she continued, "How are you feeling now?"

My stomach cramped with fear at the reality I'd never speak to my mother and brother again.

"I think I'm okay. I owe you my life for the antitoxin. I'd like to thank Dr. Volkmann, as well."

"Dr. Volkmann approved the antitoxin as a gesture of kindness toward your friend Mila. He banished her recently but regrets the decision. He wants her back as a forager as soon as possible. See, he refused to give her friend—"

"Yes, she told me about what happened. Why does Volkmann want Mila back at The Compound so badly?"

"She was a great asset to us. She can acquire anything from the island. She's the only one who can break into The Quay and steal from them. Nobody else has ever been successful. Volkmann didn't realize Mila was the one who was retrieving about 95% of the rare items we need for medicines and such. He was misinformed and would like you to assist him in getting back in Mila's good graces. He wants to offer her residency."

"Residency?"

"Not that I agree with this system, but The Compound won't allow marked people to live here - or even enter. You're the first exception I've seen in my five years. However, Volkmann employs non-violent thieves as what he calls foragers. They collect what we need in exchange for their safety from the Junk Rats, as well as a limited amount of other benefits. The foragers aren't allowed to live here, but they maintain a positive working relationship with us. Volkmann is prepared to offer Mila a home here - she can reside in The Compound, under our full protection, as long as she returns as a forager."

"Wow, well, I'm sure she will be thrilled to hear about the deal. So, do people need protection from the Junk Rats?"

"Yes, Alex. They all follow Tobias. He was once known as the I-35 Killer - I'm sure you heard of him, as he was quite famous back on the mainland."

My body shuddered at the thought of who Tobias was in his former life.

"Yes, of course. His arrest was the top news story everywhere. My mother was glued to his trial on television. He was considered the most dangerous killer who ever lived."

"When he was a free man, he murdered over two-hundred people in the span of a decade along the interstate, dumping their bodies into various lakes in Texas. He ran a cult. His followers also killed for him, kidnapped people, as well as many other heinous crimes. On the island, his disciples are the worst kind – they are cursed plagues."

"Why wasn't he put to death instead of being sent here? You would think his crimes would be enough for the death penalty, right?"

"His father was a supreme court judge. Enough said."

"Oh, I see. Well, why doesn't The Compound fight him?"

"Out of a necessary evil, The Compound has an agreement with him. We have things he needs like medical doctors and specialty food items. However, they have things we must acquire - like herbs to make antitoxin. We just can't let them know that, or we'll lose leverage. That's why we must have Mila return as a forager. We always need the upper hand, or the balance of power will turn in their favor. We have the brains; they have the brawn – and the predisposition to kill anybody who gets in their way. We have a conscience, but most of the Junk Rats wouldn't know remorse if it was their granny staring them in the face."

I wasn't sure if I should mention that Mila and I weren't friends anymore and that she would not be able to go back to The Quay to steal things for them. I kept quiet for self-preservation.

"What happened to my neck? Why'd it hurt so badly?"

"You were struck by lightning. It's a miracle. We've never saved anybody from a strike before. Typically, the chips detonate from the electrical energy. Yours malfunctioned and reflected the bolt, saving your life. I saw it happen right outside of The Compound. It was a wondrous sight - looked magical."

I dredged my fingers across the back of my neck over an open wound surrounded by raised, hardened skin. As my hand swished in front of my face, I caught a whiff of burnt flesh.

"You've got a nasty lesion back there, but it's all superficial. Good news is the chip seems to have lost power and probably won't work anymore. We think your C1 and C2 are fine. You're a lucky young man. Let's get up and walk. Dr. Volkmann requires patients of the infirmary to work for their recovery and not just lie in beds."

Modest, I glanced over at my shirt and shorts and hesitated.

"Oh, my. Sure. Here you go." She placed my folded clothes on the table beside me and stepped outside of the room. "I'll wait for you right here."

I shook out my shoulders and rolled my neck. Sore, but bearable. My leg still ached, but the rash hadn't spread. The numbness had faded, and my nerves tingled back into life. My shirt, shorts, and shoes had been cleaned, and the blood splatter stains removed.

After getting dressed, I met Nurse Rose in the hallway.

"Again, thank you for everything," I said, inhaling the first clean scent since I had stepped foot on the island.

"Do you know where Mila is? We figured she'd swing by to check on you, Alex. Our sources cannot find her."

At a loss for the right words, I stumbled.

"Um, during the storm we were separated after lightning hit the tree we were hiding in. I'm sure she'll turn up."

The nurse stared at me with an expression of concern, the lines in her forehead deepening.

"This way," she said, directing me to turn down the main hallway.

We passed by armed guards monitoring the front windows of The Compound. I had been on the other side of the reinforced wall before. I recognized the guard who had threatened to shoot me.

"Wow, that young man out there looks like your twin, Alex," Nurse Rose said as she gazed out of a window.

I stopped in my tracks and scanned the area for whom she was going on about. I choked on air as my eyes locked on Larry Bateman. My first instinct was to run outside and strangle him to death for betraying me, but I took a deep breath to calm myself. Larry was standing with a guy whose hair was the same shade of brown as mine, similar haircut, his body the same athletic build with long legs. I couldn't see his face, as he was turned the opposite direction.

"Yes, he does look like me from this point of view, that's for sure."

"Oh, you should see his face. Wait and see if he looks this way, Alex."

Larry Bateman had his next victim, probably taking this poor guy to The Quay. They had halted in front of The Compound, just out of the range of the guards. He was talking with animated hands, pointing toward the building. I recalled him giving me the same tour. The boy turned my direction. My heart stopped. My breaths turned thin as I struggled to make out the features of his face. He had two red stripes tattooed on his cheek - just like me. From what I could tell, Nurse Rose was right about him looking like my twin.

"That's, that's my brother. That's Tony, my little brother. I've got to get out of here, now."

12 TIGERS

"What do you mean, that's your brother?" Nurse Rose said with a puzzled expression on her face.

I searched for an exit, but all I could find was guarded windows.

"How do I get out of here? I have to get Tony. Now."

"Alex, if you leave the building, I cannot guarantee that Dr. Volkmann will allow you to return. Dusk is coming."

"I don't care, Nurse Rose. Get me out of here."

Feeling as if I had the revving engine of a Porsche inside my gut, I took off at full speed, scanning the corridor for the way out. My pounding heart resonated in my ears.

"The exit's over here."

Nurse Rose pointed to a narrow strip that branched from the main hallway. "I'm afraid this may be goodbye. I do wish you well."

She escorted me through two sets of doors, checking in with a guard at a small checkpoint in between.

Bursting out of The Compound, I raced toward my brother.

"Tony!"

Just as he and Larry turned to walk away, he halted, spun around, and locked eyes with me.

"Alex!"

He sped toward me as tears gushed from his eyes. I held out my hands to grasp his shoulders and pulled him in for a tight hug. Questions exploded in my head like fireworks.

"What the hell—"

Holding his shoulders, I stepped back and studied his face.

"Alex, you'll never believe what happened—"

Larry stormed over with a bowed chest, shouting. "We must go now. If you want to live, you'll stay far away from that guy, he should be dead." He glared at me. "No idea how you survived, but Tobias will be furious you're still breathing air."

Larry's eyes burned into mine. My hands balled into fists by instinct, as I wanted to punch him in the mouth with all my strength. I had never wanted to do that to anyone before.

"He's my brother," Tony said.

Larry's expression switched from confusion to anger as his eyes bounced back and forth between our faces, his nostrils flared and weathered cheeks flushed red.

"You've got to be kidding." He shook his head and swiped his hand through the unruly mop on his head. "Brothers? What are the chances?" He laughed. "Tobias will be on the warpath when he finds out you survived, Alex. No idea how you're still here, but you should run and hide. Consider that advice from a former friend."

"You're nobody's friend, you are nothing but a selfish traitor," I said, as I pulled my brother closer to me.

I took a giant step to face him as he reached behind his back and traversed around me to grab Tony. He shoved my chest to get me out of the way and, with white knuckles, he held a Bowie knife to Tony's neck. With pursed lips, he cocked a bushy eyebrow upward.

"Larry, don't do anything stupid. Put the knife down."

Tony took a sharp intake of breath, his eyelids raised and jaws clenched.

"I warned you. I advised you as a friend to get out of here. I'm delivering this boy to Tobias. He's an innocent with red stripes. Tobias won't allow impersonators to run around the island. He believes you're all spies for The Compound and must be exterminated by fight or fire. This is my last run before I'm a full-time sentry. I made it, Alex. I finally made it."

Larry's eyes were bewildered as he shoved the knife further into Tony's neck, trickles of blood oozed onto the knife's edge. Tony shut his eyes, his lips forming a straight, white line. I looked over my shoulder at the cutout windows of The Compound, but all I could see was tips of rifles. Nobody was coming to help.

"Just stop. Go. Don't hurt him, Larry. What can I

do to make you stop? Just take me and leave him alone."

Larry stomped his foot, drawing his overgrown eyebrows together. His eyes wild, resembling one of those monkey dolls that bang cymbals. A deep hatred filled my heart that I had never experienced before.

"You're the one hurting him, Alex. Look what time it is - the sun's about to set, and we've got to make it through The Hub. It'll be your fault when I'm forced to throw him to the tigers as bait to save myself. Tell him goodbye."

A tear rolled down Tony's cheek as the color drained from his face. He popped his eyes open, shooting a look of sheer panic toward me. The blade was rubbing against his throat, so he complied with Larry's every move.

"Tony, don't worry. I've got this handled. Just go with him. Take it off his neck, now."

I had to say anything to get Larry to stop. I didn't have a plan, but there was no way I was going to stand there while he killed my brother in front of me. I had a bit of time to figure out my next move.

"Don't say I didn't warn you to run, Alex."

Larry twisted Tony's arm behind his body and pressed the knife into his back, pushing him toward The Hub. There wasn't going to be enough time to make it to The Quay before dark. I was weakened by my injuries without a weapon or a plan, but I was determined. I surveyed the guards in the windows of The Compound once again, and the guns hadn't budged. They weren't going to intervene.

"Alex, move," a familiar female voice shouted from behind.

Quick footsteps hit the ground from behind me, and I spun around to lock eyes with Mila. Wide- eyed and focused, she was sprinting with a hatchet held with both hands. With a dash through the sand, she passed me and caught up to Larry. My first instinct was to shout for Tony to pull away, but I froze as I realized her objective. The next few seconds felt as if a remote control slowed the speed of my world. Nearly a foot shorter than him, she swung the weapon toward Larry's skull. I gasped for air as the metal blade connected with the base of his neck. The sound reminded me of my first home run hit in little league baseball. With the hatchet protruding from his head, he twisted around to lay eyes on his foe. He stumbled before he hit the sand, the blade furthering into his brain and blood spewing from the wound. I stood motionless.

"Holy mother of –"

"Alex, get your brother, let's go."

Tony dropped to his knees, moaning.

"Tony!" I rushed toward him as he curled into a fetal position. "What's wrong?"

Mila bowed her head without a word, pointing at the Bowie knife sticking out of his back.

"I'm fine, Alex. I'm fine," he said with tears streaming down his cheek. "Just stings a bit."

Bright red blood infused his shirt around the blade.

"I'm so sorry. I didn't see him holding that to his back. I'm so sorry," Mila said, wringing out her wrist in the air and pacing back and forth. "I swear I didn't do this on purpose, Alex."

"What should we do? Remove it? It doesn't seem to be bleeding too badly." I studied the location of the weapon. "It's not in his heart, lungs, liver. It's not centered, so it didn't land on his spinal cord, and kidneys would be down there, so it missed those too."

I had paid attention in health class because my teacher was smoking hot.

"It appears to be in *No Man's Land*. Soft tissue would be right there, I think, but I don't think you're supposed to remove it, Alex. Let me get the surgeon. Good thing we're at The Compound. There are people who can help right behind those walls."

"It's nearly dark. A nurse said I couldn't go back in there if I left, so where should I set up camp? I don't have any tiger repellent, is that okay?"

My mind was spinning. Larry's body was awkwardly posed, his mouth ajar as his blank eyes stared at me.

"I'll be right back, Alex. We can either make a deal to stay at The Compound or go to Mila's Grove – as long as we're moving away from The Hub as soon as possible, it should be fine. If this is your brother, I know he'll keep my secret. I've thought about what happened at The Quay, and I'm sorry I acted the way I did. I do trust you. He betrayed both of us." She pointed at Larry. "We're friends, if that's okay with you."

"Of course. Alright, see if you can get help, and please hurry. I'll just make a spot over there, under the tree. I figure we're close enough to The Compound, and the guards may show mercy and assist us if we get into trouble once they speak to you."

Tony groaned as I guided him toward a large palm tree. Larry's stiffened expression continued to stare at us as if his dead body judged our every move. Mila rushed to The Compound, and it was a couple of minutes before they sent a guard to escort her inside. I believed it to be a good sign at the time.

"Alex, I'm tired. Can I rest for a few?" Tony said with drooped eyelids as he lay on his side in the sand.

"Hold on. I have to dig holes for us. It's just how you do things here at night."

I scooped out a shallow grave in the sand, forming a pillow for his head. Tony was nearly passed out by the time I helped him into the burrow, leaving the wound with the weapon exposed. He hadn't lost too much blood, but the blade was securely embedded into his flank.

"You okay? It's not your warm bed at home, but it'll get you through the night. We'll fix this, don't worry. How do you feel? Does it hurt?"

"It throbs, but I'm getting used to it. I just haven't slept since this all happened. I'm tired, starving."

"Get some rest, brother. Mila will be back in a second and take us inside to the surgeon. He'll fix you up. They'll feed us because they want her to work for them. She has the upper hand."

After about ten minutes of sitting in silence, I had nearly forgotten about Larry's body on the ground, only a stone's throw away. In an ironic twist, I remembered how he had warned that freshly dead and injured bodies served as tiger bait. As we weren't too far from The Hub, I realized I had to remove the corpse, or we'd have company when the moon emerged. Figuring Mila would retrieve Tony in a matter of minutes, I gave him instructions to remain in place until I returned - albeit, he may have already fallen asleep, I was unsure.

"Alright, Alex," I spoke aloud to bolster my confidence. "You can do this."

I gripped the handle of the hatchet and yanked it loose from Larry's skull. Pieces of brain and oozing blood spilled out onto the sand. My stomach lurched, but I calmed it by forcing hard swallows. After tossing the weapon aside, I grabbed the ankles and dragged the body behind me.

I struggled with remembering the geography of the island. *Dead bodies belong in the Battlefield. It's between The Compound and The Quay, to the left of The Hub. It has toxic waste and pedophiles, the acid faces.* I recalled what I had been told as the sun plummeted from the sky.

I spoke aloud to boost my confidence. "I'll drop him off at the edge of the Battlefield and run back, tell the guards I'm with Mila and Tony, and it'll be fine."

After dragging the body for over a mile, the skyline turned an ominous orange, and the luminous moon discharged its ascension.

"Hey," from a few yards ahead a deep voice sounded.

The blood drained from my face as I gasped. With

nothing to protect me but a corpse, I stopped.

"What do you think you're doing?"

He pushed his mottled face within an inch of mine, his smooth, ridged skin glistening from the last rays of the setting sun. He was an acid face, a pedophile. His presence and the hint of a rotting stench confirmed I had gone far enough.

"Nothing. I mean, I found this body, and I'm taking it to the Battlefield where it belongs."

With a casual motion, I dropped Larry's ankles and spun around to run away. The fiend grabbed me by the shoulders and moved in closer. His hand bore into my flesh with an iron grip.

"No, you're coming with me to pay your penance. This isn't where you dump corpses to rot."

"I'm not going anywhere with you, man."

I attempted to shrug out of his hold, but he outsized me and clenched my shoulders tighter. From the direction of The Hub, pounding footsteps sounded. Five silhouettes marched our way in a V formation. Junk Rats.

The acid-faced man released my shoulder and turned to escape. A Junk Rat lunged for him, stabbing him in the back with a sword while another shot an arrow into the side of his head. The first man twisted the blade as he pulled it out, his lips twitching into a smile as he shoved the man toward the ground. He wiped the blood from the knife onto his pants and slid it back into a belted holster. The frontman, bald with skin the color of a milk chocolate bar, stopped the formation a few feet away.

"State your purpose."

He lowered his gaze to Larry's body crumpled behind me.

"Um, well, there was an accident, and he didn't make it."

The two Junk Rats flanking their frontman ambled over toward the body and flipped him over. His face wore a frozen, stunned expression with eyes staring straight ahead.

"That's Bateman," a stocky guy with red hair said, before marching toward me to glare into my eyes. "And you're the dude who broke into The Quay with that thief girl. You were supposed to be taken to the cages. You're supposed to be dead." He wrapped his hand around my neck and squeezed. "You killed our new sentry!"

Choking, I struggled for air as I grabbed at his fingers to release them. A giant silhouette in the back of the V stepped forward, his beard was shaggy and face weathered. It was Joe from the Texas prison. He gave me a suspicious look with his one good eye and nodded before he returned to his position. My chest heaved for breath. I resorted to using my fingernails on the Junk Rat's hand, and he increased the pressure.

"Let him go. We must take him to Tobias at once," the bald man said. "You've killed his newest recruit. I'm unsure of your fate, but it's likely fight or fire."

The hand liberated my neck, and I gasped for air.

"Why don't we just kill him? Bring his head back to Tobias," a short ginger said.

"He's tall, bulky, a good candidate for the ring.

He's a survivor," the leader said. "We do as directed and bring insurgents to Tobias."

Thunderous growls echoed from the direction of The Hub.

"Weapons out," the bald man shouted.

They pulled out an assortment of weapons from holsters and turned toward The Hub. Whatever they were doing, they had done it before.

"Secure the insurgent," the leader said.

Joe put a massive hand on my shoulder and guided me to stand inside of their formation.

"But, is that a tiger? Shouldn't we get out of here?" I said, my feet like bricks as we started progressing toward the sound.

The moon had ascended, and the orange sky had metamorphosed into a brilliant blue. The tigers traversed the steep rocks on the side of The Hub effortlessly and lunged onto the sand - deadly but majestic as their moving shadows hurried toward us. My muscles tightened, and sweat poured from my pores as I readied myself for the inevitable.

"In position," the leader said as he lowered to a knee.

He wielded a machete with two hands in front of his chest. The others dropped in position holding their weapon of choice - a bow and arrow, a mace, and a long sword. Joe put a strong hand on my shoulder and held an axe in his other. In a state of terror, my knees locked and I stood rigid, swaying in place.

"Stay strong, men. Straight to the throat, deep slice."

An unhinged tiger bound our way at an incredible speed, headed for the frontman. An arrow caught the cat in the neck, but she was unfazed. She sprang into the air, paws spread wide and teeth gnashing. With a growling roar, she crushed into the bald man's shoulders, driving him into the ground as a second arrow penetrated her back. The machete flew from his hands as the beast tore into his neck with a side-to-side motion. A mace smacked the side of the tiger's head, but she continued to mangle her prey savagely. Screams of agony pierced my eardrums as the frontman punched at the tiger. All efforts to survive were futile.

"Get ready," the little ginger with the long sword said. He rose as a second tiger sailed toward him.

With a warrior-yell that flowed through me like a shard of glass, the redhead swung his sword in a strong arch, slicing the pulp of the tiger's throat as an arrow landed between the beast's eyes. Deep crimson blood gushed in a wave, coating the swordsman like Carrie at the prom. The five hundred pound brute crashed into the sand beside him and rolled a few feet away. The bloodied man soared onto the tiger's belly and plunged his sword into his chest to finish him off. Another tiger pounced on the mace handler, taking arrows in his flank as if they were nothing. The first tiger grabbed her lifeless prey by the neck and moved outside of the fray. Joe didn't move. Adrenaline pummeled me from the inside - fight or flight, champion or deserter - I was a spectator with a front row view and no plan to defend myself. The heavy iron ball covered in spikes crashed against the cat's head, and the animal grumbled ferociously and countered with a massive paw across the mace handler's face, talons ripping the flesh from his cheek. The bloody ginger left his kill and assisted his comrade, gouging the tiger in the side until the wounded animal retreated into the shadows.

The bald man's body was limp as his attacker dragged him away into the darkness. Joe didn't move. With another tiger springing toward us, my survival instinct kicked in, and I snapped out of my catatonic trance. Tony needed me, and I wasn't going to die this way. I glanced at Joe to gauge his reaction and shrugged away from his grip as the mace connected with the fourth tiger's head. Joe didn't react. My feet dug into the stand as I twisted around and ran as fast as my legs could carry me toward The Compound. I never looked back.

13 SAVING TONY

Determined and alone, my feet pounded against the sand in the dark of the night. I imagined Tony bandaged up, enjoying a hot meal as Mila waited for me in front of the building. On impulse, I slowed down as a shadow marched toward me in the distance. The silhouette held large bags on either side. I planned a casual pass by without a word. We drew closer. My heart palpitated as a flashlight shined directly in my face.

"You're that kid," the figure said from a few feet away.

He grabbed my arm as we crossed paths, dropping his flashlight on the ground. A familiar smell of pungent fish assaulted my nose.

"I have to go," I said, wriggling out of his grip.

"No, you're coming with me. You owe me."

It was Dirty Pete. He blocked my path and yanked me back in the direction that I had just traveled. Under the moonlight, the gaping hole in his face appeared black. He was monstrous.

"I wouldn't go that way. There are tigers attacking some Junk Rats. I saved you. Now we're even."

I jerked my shoulder from his grip. He wiped his

nose on the back of his hand and shook his head, laughing.

"Happens all the time, tell me something I haven't heard. I'm solving a big problem on the island, and you're gonna help. You owe me."

He waved his wrist stump in front of my face.

Curiosity got a hold of me. "What problem are you solving?"

Tiger growls echoed in the distance. I hadn't made it far enough away. We'd be their next meal if the Junk Rats lost the battle. Dirty Pete didn't react to the tigers. He either was unhinged crazy or had a surefire method to defeat the beasts.

"I'm burning down The Hub. I know we need some stuff that grows on the trees there, but I'll tell ya what we don't need - those dumb cats attacking us every night. I get rid of their home, they've got nowhere to hide out during the day, and we can take 'em out. But my bigger reason is that the Junk Rats took my eye and hand, and I'm gettin' revenge. I'm sick of those freaks killing everybody who goes into The Hub and terrorizing folks on the island. We need to even the playing field a bit. I'm taking their cover away."

Pete was an arsonist. A vengeful arsonist. I had no time for him.

"Look, do what you have to do, Pete. But I have to get back to The Compound. I won't say a word about this to anybody."

Pete dropped his bag and pulled out his serrated knife he had used on me once before. He only had one hand and was missing an eye, so I knew I could take him. Without deliberation, I coldcocked him in his jaw. A huge grin grew on my face as he tumbled and splayed onto the ground, bewildered. I kicked his bags as far as I could before turning to run back to Tony. I was younger, stronger, and knew I could outrun him.

My feet never stopped running until I made it back to The Compound. I was sad to find Tony fast asleep in the burrow underneath the tree. I leaned down, my eyes following the movements of his chest. He was still breathing. The island was still, silent, but the rifles of The Compound's front wall remained poised on the front windowsills. I wondered where Mila was, hoping she hadn't betrayed us.

"Alex?" Tony said.

He stirred in his sandy bed with contracted brows.

"Yeah, I'm here, bud. How do you feel?"

"My back hurts," he said.

As he tried rolling over, I grabbed his arm and pulled him upright. He had forgotten where he was and that he had a knife sticking out of his back. He groaned.

"Be careful, man. Remember you got that."

I pointed to his wound. He nodded and stared at the moon, positioning himself in the sand. He groaned again.

"Ah, yes." His speech was slowed. He twisted his body and peered at the knife. "Thought all that was a dream for a sec." He forced a laugh. "It got dark, huh?"

"Yeah, it's getting late. Do you know if Mila's been out here?"

"Last thing I can recall is you telling me to stay here. I slept until now."

After surveying The Compound, I concluded there was no activity inside. Whatever Mila had worked out with them must not have included urgent care for Tony.

"Is that a fire over there?

I swiveled around to see a ball of fire in the distance, a plume of dark smoke rising into the dark blue sky.

"Well, Dirty Pete must've already set The Hub on fire. This should be interesting."

"Dirty Pete?"

"Long story. He's nuts. I'll catch you up on that later. More importantly, how did you get in this place? You've got red stripes on your face - who'd you kill?"

He swiped his hand across his cheek.

"I have *red stripes*?"

"They tattoo your face on the ship - the ship that brought you to the island."

"So that's what they were doing. Man, that hurt," he said.

"They didn't put you asleep? They gave me an injection, and I woke up later - never knew they did it."

"Must be nice. Wonder why you got special treatment? Maybe that stupid judge felt sorry."

"Yeah, he had to know I was innocent, right? So,

tell me. Why are you here?"

I scooped sand around his legs to cover them as he braced himself on the palm tree with his good side.

"I did research about what you told me. License plate GLC889, a black Lincoln Town Car." He paused to change positioning. After taking a deep pain-managing breath, he continued. "It was the strangest thing - every title search, license plate search, VIN search was blocked. Mom and I hired a private investigator with the reverse mortgage money we raised for your defense - which we never had the chance to use, as you know. The PI found the owner of the car."

He pursed his lips and narrowed his eyes.

"And?"

He sighed.

"The car was registered to Walter Glasgow of Odessa, Texas."

I stared in the shadows, trying to figure out what the significance of this man could be.

"Why does that name sound familiar?"

I pondered the name while my brother bowed his head, slowly shaking it from side to side.

"It was the judge. The one who put you here, Alex. Judge Glasgow - the dude with the black glasses and fat face."

Swallowing hard lumps, I stopped to draw a deep breath.

"W-What?"

"Yes, the judge that sped up your trial and threw you on this island."

My insides turned into ice, the heavy lemon scent of the courtroom became apparent as my brain tossed me back in the seat at the long table, my mother crying on the bench behind me. I looked into the judge's beady eyes, my hands trembled, and eyes dilated until they hurt. My head pounded, aching like a hammer was beating it.

"Did you kill him?"

I heard my heart beating as if a speaker played it next to my eardrum.

"No, of course not. I'm unsure how I'm here. I went to the police station to report what the PI had found. After a few minutes of waiting, they arrested me for the murder of a homeless man. Just like you, I had an expedited trial, and they produced fake witnesses."

I pressed flat palms against my eyes so hard I saw sparks.

"God, that's horrible. How's Mom? I'm sure this must have killed her."

"She seemed strong, believe it or not. Her last words were that she'd see us both soon."

"She's going to kill him. Great, I'll have two of you to worry about over here."

The fire in The Hub spread into a dull roar, smoke flying up toward a cloudless sky. Nobody stirred from within The Compound.

"Shouldn't we just pull this knife out? It's obviously not in a dangerous spot, and I don't think it's bleeding anymore, my shirt feels dry. If it were fatal, I wouldn't still be here."

I drew in a calming breath through my nostrils,

allowing my lungs to fill before I exhaled slowly.

"No, I've always heard not to pull it out. Let's at least wait until morning so you can heal around it."

"Won't it get infected?"

I shrugged. "I wish I knew the answers, man. I wonder what's going on with Mila."

As soon as I said her name, she pushed out the front door of The Compound.

"Oh, thank God." I let out an overly-exaggerated sigh as I jumped to my feet. It was the dark of night, but it appeared as though she had a couple of deep gashes on her face as she stepped toward us.

"They marked me, Alex. They marked me for murder. They saw the whole thing with Larry."

"Wait. They tattooed your face with red marks?"

"Yep."

I strained to view her cheek in the soft moonlight. Her mark was identical to Tony's, and I assumed, the same as mine.

"They told me they respected you, needed you, and wanted you to return as a forager and live in The Compound. I'm so confused."

"That was before I was a murderer. They don't work with violent people."

I clenched my jaw, finding it difficult not to start screaming and tearing the front of The Compound apart. I paced back and forth, slowing my breaths.

"What about Tony? What do we do?"

The veins in my neck pulsated.

"I've taken care of it, Alex. Let's go inside."

"Wait, what? We can go inside?"

I tilted my head and widened my eyes. She gestured for me to help my brother out of the sand pit. Without another word, we rushed him to the door of The Compound.

"It's Mila," she said, pounding on the door.

Wrathful flames engulfed The Hub as the aroma of a bonfire coated the night air. The door of The Compound creaked open. The guard invited us inside.

14 THE DEAL

The interior of The Compound was unnervingly silent. The guards sported all black attire and were stationed every ten feet along the front wall. They perched on stools, still as mannequins, with their rifles hoisted on their shoulders, the tips of their guns resting on the windowsills. Sconces holding thick candles lined the corridor behind them, all with flickering flames.

"Are we going to see the surgeon?"

"Stay quiet and walk lightly," she whispered.

I had a feeling the trip inside wasn't sanctioned by Dr. Volkmann.

We turned the corner. I recognized the route to the infirmary.

"In here," Mila said.

She pushed open a wooden door, and we walked into a room with a large surgical table in the center.

"Lay him down on his side," Nurse Rose said, walking out of the shadows.

She had a red liquid inside of a beaker. It looked like blood.

"Carefully remove his shirt, please."

We unbuttoned the front of his handmade silk shirt

and slipped it off, draping it over a chair. It was obvious Larry had taken him to Mark the tailor upon his arrival to the island.

She poured the red liquid over the wound and gently glided the knife out of his flank. Tony made a quick gasp for air, followed by a groan.

"Are you doing alright, young man?"

He winced and exhaled.

"Yes. Yes, I'm good."

"Boy, you look an awful lot like your brother," Nurse Rose said.

"We hear that quite often," I said.

She leaned in close to the open wound, examining it as carefully as she could, wiping the blood away as it emerged.

"You may be as lucky as your brother in dodging disaster. It appears as though the knife only punctured layers of muscle - your intestines don't seem to be affected. I'll clean this up and get you on your way."

The nurse poured a transparent substance over the wound and grabbed a needle and thread.

"So, he'll be okay?" Mila asked.

Mila peered outside of the door into the foyer of the infirmary and then shut the door.

"Yes, he'll be just fine. Sore, but he'll live. I'll stitch him up in a jiffy - it's not deep enough to have to keep it open and packed. Thank God for dull knives, huh?"

"Speaking of knives, hand that over, please," Mila said with a smile.

I leaned over, grabbed it, and gave it to her.

"Oh, dear. I cannot believe they did that to your beautiful face," the nurse said to Mila.

"Well, I did kill someone. They were just following the rules, you know."

"I'm so sorry about that. Some of the rules here are so stupid." She shook her head and sighed. "I'd like to keep him here for twenty-four hours and administer antibiotic therapy. Most people don't die on the battlefield from their wounds, but rather from infection. It's not like your assailant stabbed you with a sterile blade."

"But, is that okay? I mean, Mila had us sneak in here. Won't you get into trouble for having a Red Stripe in here?"

"Alex, we only snuck in here because others are sleeping. Just being courteous. This is on the up and up. The surgeon's on-call if needed, but Nurse Rose has military experience with knife wounds such as this - she was the best for the job."

"Ah, I see. Well, that sounds like a plan."

Mila smiled. "Tony can stay in here, hooked to an IV, and Nurse Rose will show us to our rooms. You and Tony were given a one-night stay."

"So that's what took so long - you worked it all out, huh? Thank you so much, it means the world."

"Mila's the best, isn't she?" Nurse Rose said as she inserted the needled into Tony's arm and hooked his IV bag on a stand next to the table.

"Yes, she is."

"I just know what they need, and I made them a deal they couldn't refuse. The negotiations are what took time," Mila said.

Guilt consumed me for doubting Mila. We said goodnight to him and tiptoed through the dimly-lit corridors toward the dorm suite. The rooms were labeled. She opened door C and ushered us inside. It was a tiny room without a window, and there was a skinny bunk bed.

Mila ignited the gas lamp on the wall, lowering it to a dim flicker. I had detected a faint burning aroma inside of the structure upon arrival, and it was becoming more evident. It was the growing forest fire. We pondered the sleeping arrangement for a moment. Mila climbed onto the top bunk, so I crawled onto the bottom bed. It was heaven to feel a mattress covered with soft, silky sheets, even if I was too tall and my feet were exposed. However, this wasn't a bed I would have considered comfortable back home. Comfort was relative.

"Did you speak to Dr. Volkmann when you came in here?"

The dancing flame on the wall was mesmerizing.

"Nobody talks directly to Dr. Volkmann. But I spoke to his right hand, the surgeon, Dr. Rose."

"Rose? You mean Nurse Rose?"

"No, silly. The surgeon's her husband."

"Oh, I see. So, are people trustworthy here or not? I've met Nurse Rose, and she seems legit."

"I was banished from this group for trying to save my best friend's life. They look out for their best interests. If you have the same interests and they need you, then, yeah, you can trust them."

"And if they don't need you?"

"Don't believe a word they say. Now that Tony's here, you'll have to protect him. He seems more naïve than you are. Is he younger?"

"By less than a year, but yes."

"Always remember where Mila's Grove is, on the other side of Purgatory."

"Maybe we can build a house over on that side of the island and fortify it like The Compound? Us three can live there," I said.

Mila giggled. I hadn't thought what I said was funny, but left it alone, nevertheless.

"So you've never told me. Why'd you get sent here?"

Silence arose for a long minute. For a moment, I thought she had passed out, but then she exhaled.

"It was so stupid, Alex. My best friend, Annie, got into a big argument with this girl named Sophia. Annie's ring was stolen from her gym locker, and she just knew Sophia had lifted it because she never showed up to gym class but was at school that day."

"Wait, so you were sent here because someone stole something from your friend?"

Patience wasn't one of my personality traits.

"No. She had the silly idea to break into this girl's house the following day during school hours to get her jewelry back. The ring meant a lot to her since it was a family heirloom."

"Don't tell me you went along with this."

"I did. She was very convincing and had a foolproof plan - or so we thought."

"You were caught, obviously?"

"To shorten the story, yeah, we were. Everything went according to plan. We entered through an unlocked door in the back, found the ring on her dresser, and that's when things went wrong." She sighed. "Her house had motion sensitive cameras monitored by an alarm company. They called the police and triggered a lockdown mode so we couldn't escape. We were arrested. The cops didn't even care to hear our side of the story."

"No way."

"Wanna hear the worst part of it all?"

"I can't imagine what could be worse."

"Annie had to return her family heirloom to Sophia."

"That's despicable. Then you guys were both sent here for life. But you were still in high school?"

"Yes, we were seventeen, but were put on trial as adults. Our case was heard forty-eight hours after the arrest, and we were here the following day. Our parents didn't even have time to get an attorney or arrange a defense."

"That sounds quite familiar." I moaned in disgust. "Mila, I'm sorry to hear that. And I'm still sad about how Annie died – especially since they saved me from the same fate. I hate to say it, but the people here seem pretty cool. I'm thankful for what they've done for me."

"As I said before, don't trust anybody. Nurse Rose's a good person, though. She's the one who let me sneak in to try and steal the antitoxin for Annie.

Her husband caught me, but I didn't rat her out."

Hearing Mila's story made me feel closer to her, and far less alone than I had felt before.

"Oh, almost forgot. Dirty Pete started the fire on The Hub. Can you smell it in here or am I imagining it?"

"Yeah, it smells like something's burning, for sure. Doesn't surprise me one bit - he's an arsonist."

A few minutes passed, and I grew sleepy, hypnotized by the tiny flame in the gas lamp casting dancing shadows upon the wall.

"Are you going to live in The Compound and work for them as a forager now? Nurse Rose told me how badly they wanted you back."

"Not exactly, Alex. Don't worry about it, though. I've made a deal. Your brother will be treated, and we get to stay the night tonight, protected by The Compound. That's all you need to know. Remember how I said I wished someone would have sheltered me from knowing all I know about Dregs Island?"

"Mila, we're friends. Please don't take on a burden for me."

"Alex, we *are* friends. Goodnight."

15 THE PLAN

The flame of the gas lamp had burned out by the time I awoke, disoriented from the dark room. From down the corridor, there were rumblings of voices and footsteps. I figured the sun had risen as I inhaled the stale smoke-coated air.

"You up?"

Silence.

"Mila?"

I tossed the sheets to the side and crawled out of the bunk.

"Mila," I said.

Her bed was made. She was gone. I took a few steps into the corridor. Nurse Rose spotted me and rushed over.

"Alex, you're awake. Would you like to see Tony? He's doing much better."

I wondered if Nurse Rose ever slept as I followed her into the infirmary. Tony had been moved into the room I had been in with my neck injury. He was lying on the table with an IV still in his arm, staring at the wall.

"Hey, man. How's it going?"

He smiled. "Hey, bro. Had a bit of a rough night,"

he said as he pointed to the IV bag. "I got a fever, and she increased the dose."

I stared at the nurse, awaiting her reassurance he was alright.

"Completely expected, Alex. Don't fret. That's exactly why I didn't release him last night. He'll be good as new soon."

A dark-complexioned man strode in, wearing a pair of homemade scrubs. His dark eyes were small and placed farther apart than usual, sitting below bushy eyebrows. His ears protruded at ninety-degree angles from his head.

"Hello, dear," Nurse Rose said.

He kissed her on the cheek and moved toward Tony.

It was Dr. Rose, the surgeon.

"How does your wound feel?"

He removed the bandage and inspected the injury. Nurse Rose had done a well-ordered job on the stitches.

"It's sore, but not throbbing anymore."

He pulled an old mercury thermometer from the cabinet and stuck it underneath Tony's tongue as he rolled him back onto his back. After a few minutes, he inspected it and then tossed it in the drawer.

"It's down to 101.5. Not terrible. Maybe switch to the stronger stuff, Natalie."

"Will do."

She grabbed a syringe from the drawer, and filled it from a vial on the shelf behind her. Then, she stuck the needle into an apparatus connected to the IV tube and adjusted a dial.

"Do you guys know where Mila went?"

Nurse Rose and her husband exchanged glances. For a moment, I became suspicious, but as soon as she spoke, the feeling waned.

"Well, as you know, Mila worked out a deal with Dr. Volkmann. She's retrieving supplies for us. However, The Hub was burned down last night, so she has her work cut out for her. Hopefully, she can still find some of the essential plants we need."

"The Hub's gone? Completely? I saw when it first caught fire last night."

Dr. Rose swished his head around and stared at me with his small eyes.

"Do you know who's responsible? Did you see who did it?"

"No, just saw it from right outside of the building last night."

I thought it was best not to tell on Dirty Pete.

"Do you guys think Dr. Volkmann would ever wage war on The Quay? With The Hub down, they don't have anything safeguarding their area. From what I've gathered, they relied upon the cover The Hub gave them, right? Are they vulnerable now?"

The surgeon tilted his head to the side and studied me. At that moment, I realized I should limit my words.

"That goes both ways, Alex. They can also see you coming," Nurse Rose said. "But it's true they can't ambush you now."

Tony scowled, obviously confused by the

conversation.

"I was just wondering if it would be worth my time to assemble an army with some people in Purgatory. I know The Compound only engages in defensive strategies, but what if I was able to recruit enough people to take over The Quay. Would The Compound take my side, do you think?"

Dr. Rose gazed at me for a long moment before there was a slight upturn in his lips.

"Possibly, young man. It would depend on what you can offer us. At this time, we have a treaty with Tobias that must be upheld. However, we've recently had to amend our agreement, as we just discovered that Mila was caught breaking into their territory and Tobias found out she worked for us. That was a bad blow."

My eyes drew to the ground for a few seconds, as I tried to blank my expression. I hadn't divulged that information, so they had heard it elsewhere. I had been in The Compound after the incident and had feigned ignorance. I hoped they weren't aware of that fact.

"In your opinion, do you think, if organized appropriately, the people of Purgatory could take over The Quay?"

The room quieted. Tony shot me a look of concern, and I questioned whether I was making a colossal mistake by divulging my thoughts. Mila had warned me not to trust anybody in The Compound. Dr. Rose finally broke the silence.

"The people of Purgatory have been tortured by

Tobias's people for many years. They are intimidated, consistently maimed, and lose loved ones on a daily basis - yet, their numbers remain greatest on the island. The right person could lead them to take over The Quay and overthrow Tobias. However, the problem with this faction is that they are primarily made up of the mentally unstable. It would be an impossible challenge to attempt to control them in a combat situation."

Tony stared into my eyes and nodded. He agreed it had to be done.

"How much longer does he need to be on the medicine?" I asked.

"Until dusk at a minimum."

"Thank you, Dr. and Nurse Rose for everything you are doing for Tony. I appreciate you so much. Tony, get some rest, I'll be back at dusk."

16 HERMAN

I scurried through the corridor and exited The Compound. Marching toward Purgatory, I formulated my plan. I was a Red Stripe. The people there were unsettled by my mark, so I planned to use it to my advantage. Tobias feared impersonators of The Quay, so I figured I would rationalize his fear. I avoided the area of huts where I had witnessed a beheading, hoping to locate a section of at least semi-sane residents. I snaked my way through the village and stumbled upon a well-built cabin with vegetation planted in the front. I climbed onto the porch and lightly knocked on the door.

"Who is it?" a male voice said.

"I wish to speak to you about something very important."

"What's so important?"

Spotting a fluttering movement through the peephole in the door, I turned my cheek the other way so he could see my mark. I figured I'd get straight to the point.

"I want to take down Tobias and dissolve The Quay."

Silence arose other than voices chattering in the

distance and birds singing above.

"You're a Red Stripe. A Junk Rat. You're a traitor. I don't trust traitors. Just as you are betraying your leader, you will betray me – a complete stranger."

"That's my point. I'm not one of them. They are evil and need to be eradicated. Open the door."

"How are you not a Junk Rat with those marks on your face?"

"Please, let me in and let's talk. I mean you no harm. Let me propose my plan. If you disagree, I'll be on my way."

Another bout of unnerving silence followed before he twisted the door handle and pushed it open. He was a petite middle-aged man with a rounded belly and hair haloed around his head with a few lone wisps crowning the top. His plump nose was shaped like a pear.

"Come in, have a seat."

"My name is Alex Cardin. And you?"

"Herman."

A pleasant cedar aroma filled the room. A small fireplace made up the back wall with a large duct piped into the ceiling. There were two woody beds on either side with tiger pelts draped across them. The sandy floor had smooth pebbles scattered about, and the wooden plank walls angled in toward the A-line ceiling. Cozy, yet confining.

"You've done an excellent job building this place, Herman."

"My wife and I built it when we first got to the island six years ago."

He gazed at the ground for a moment before taking a seat on one of the beds. He gestured to the other bed, and I lowered myself onto it.

"Your wife? Where's she?"

"Junk Rats took her during one of their patrols in Purgatory about three years ago. She's most likely gone by now."

I noticed his right hand was missing. A thief. Most people are right-handed, so he was possibly violent.

"I hate to hear that. Well, that's why I'm here. I think they have to be stopped."

"Why me? Why did you choose me of all people in Purgatory?"

After gazing at the ceiling to select the appropriate words, I locked eyes with him.

"I'm just going to be honest. You have a nicely built house. That speaks sanity to me. I need someone sane to speak to about this. I need a right-hand man who I can trust in battle."

He thinned his lips into a line and shook his head.

"Do you know how strong they are? They are all crazy." He paused for a moment as he shot his eyes toward the ceiling. "I could tell them your plan and receive a month's reward of protection, you know."

"But you won't do that. You fear them, but you hate them. You want revenge for what they did to you and your wife. You want the terror to stop."

Herman grinned. This wasn't a cheerful conversation. This man was crazy.

"You've got me wrong. I don't want to be your ally. I don't want any part of this, and if you say one more word to me about it, I will go straight to Tobias and give him the news in exchange for a temporary peace of mind. You will never take him down. Learn to live with how things are on this island."

I bowed my head, swishing my foot back and forth in the sand.

"You're making a mistake."

Herman rose and marched toward the door. "It's about time for their afternoon patrol. You need to leave now."

I exited Herman's house and walked around Purgatory, knocking on a few more doors of sturdy domiciles. Every person gave me the same reaction. I was about to give up the quest when I locked eyes with the small Asian tailor.

"Mark," I shouted as I ran toward him.

He waited for me, peering over his glasses.

"Yes, what can I do for you?"

He held a halved coconut. He popped a chunk into his mouth.

"I have something important to discuss. Can we go somewhere and talk in private?"

"You don't look like you have anything to trade, and you already have clothes. What do you want with me?"

"It isn't something to talk about in the open. Just give me a few minutes."

"Where's Larry? Last time I saw you, he was escorting you to The Quay. Are you with Tobias now?"

"That's a long story. Please, just give me a few

minutes to explain everything. You seem like a reasonable person. I think you'll like what I have to say."

Mark glared at me for what seemed like forever before he sighed.

"Let's go to my place," he said.

We strolled to his hut, and he invited me inside. The interior was bigger than the cabin I had just visited, with beautiful silk tapestries hanging on the walls and colorful pillows scattered on the couch and bed. On the ground was a woven silk rug.

"Take a seat anywhere. Would you like a coconut?"

"Yes, please. I haven't had anything in quite some time."

I accepted his offering and pulled off a piece. I swallowed it without chewing because I was famished.

"So what is the big story? Alex, right?"

I lowered onto the couch, and he took his wooden chair by the table.

"Yes, sir."

After divulging my plan of taking over The Quay, we stared at each other for a minute. With pursed lips, he shot a glance toward the ceiling but appeared to be surprisingly receptive. I was glad he didn't mention Larry again at that time.

"To be honest, I've waited to meet someone like you." I wanted to scream for joy but kept silent. "I've already assembled a group of rebels, but we've never had a strong frontman. I'm no leader, but I have a secret weapon I've been working on for two years. It's ready." He smiled, and I countered with the biggest grin I had pulled off since my arrival on the island. "Meet me in the back of Purgatory in fifteen minutes. I'll gather the ones I trust, and we'll discuss how we can accomplish this goal."

I agreed, shook his hand, and set off toward the shore. For a moment, I considered popping into Mila's Grove for a few mangoes, but there wasn't quite enough time and didn't want to risk being caught coming from that direction. I reached the beach early, so I made a seat in the sand and leaned against a palm tree trunk. I closed my eyes and enjoyed the gentle breeze while inhaling the clean, salty air. My ears soothed from the relaxing waves of the ocean. Then, my eyes popped open. Catching sight of the guard towers, thoughts of paradise erased from my mind. Further down the shore, two men were pulling a shark across the sand by a fishing line. Vivid images of the snapping teeth of hungry sharks brought me further back into my nightmarish reality. I tried closing my eyes again, but the moment was tainted. A few minutes later, a parade of about fifteen people ventured to the shore with Mark. He had introduced each one before they sat down in the sand in front of me.

"Alex has a plan to take over Tobias. Let's listen to what he has to say and then discuss."

My nerve endings exploded like fireworks, as I had never taken on this much responsibility in my life. The only time I'd addressed a group was the year before while presenting my history report to the class.

At an instant, all eyes were on me, so I swallowed hard, cleared my throat, and kept my chin up.

"Um, as Mark said, I want to take down Tobias. His Junk Rats terrorize the people in Purgatory every day. Purgatory is the largest sector of Dregs." I sounded like I was reading a history report. I knew I needed to be more motivating to inspire an army, so I ramped up my cadence. "The intimidation and violence must stop. Tobias and the Junk Rats will no longer rule this island." Soft clapping erupted with nods of agreement. "To accomplish this, we need to recruit more people. We need strong people like you. There's strength in numbers. The Compound has agreed to stay out of it, even though they have a treaty with The Quay. However, they've promised to sign a deal with us once we disband The Quay."

A lady with stringy blond hair wearing a pink dress raised her hand, her arm severely burned. I nodded at her to speak.

"Alex, they're all murderers. They kill without remorse. We may have numbers, but they're of a different world. They may even have weapons for all we know."

A few voices affirmed her words. All eyes focused on me. I stopped breathing for a short moment as I remembered the weapon bunker. They did have an arsenal, and it was my fault.

"It doesn't matter if they have weapons. We need to take them by surprise before they can use them. I had a friend who was breaking into The Quay on a daily basis and stealing items for The Compound. It can be done. They aren't very smart."

A thin man with a sad face raised a bony hand. I acknowledged him.

"I can get twenty more people, but that's it. How about everybody else? What's our count?"

After sorting it all out, we figured we had over two hundred people as definite, with the possibility of recruiting over a thousand, possibly more. We reasoned there were nearly five hundred Junk Rats in The Quay. We had to recruit at least double, maybe even triple to accomplish our goals – or be able to take down a large part of their population at once by clever means.

"Alex, may I have the floor?" Mark said.

"Certainly."

He stood in front of the group and pulled a vial of green liquid from his pocket, waving it in the air.

"This is the answer." Gasps and moans followed. "I stumbled upon this herb during the early years of formulating dyes for my clothes. In diluted solutions, it made my hand numb for hours. I figured out how to concentrate it and discovered it's a paralytic - a very potent one."

"Is that all you have, Mark, in that vial? It doesn't seem like very much," a dark-skinned man said.

"Yes, it has taken me three years to make this much. It is a painstaking process to extract the toxin and concentrate it. However, only a minuscule amount is needed for full paralysis."

"How do you know that?" I asked.

"I started with animals, Alex. I stumbled upon a

litter of tiger cubs and used them to perform tests. They don't seem to mind it and just go to sleep. The tigers are grown now, and consider me a friend - so I don't think I made them too mad with my experiments."

Soft chuckles erupted.

"Don't paralytics kill? Like, stopping the heart?" I asked.

"Not this one, it only paralyzes skeletal muscle - smooth and cardiac muscle are not affected."

"Where are these tigers, Mark?" the thin, sad man said.

"I've got a secret den for them in the uninhabited part of Dregs. They don't harm humans unless I'm threatened. I keep them well fed with shark meat, but I've found them to be quite protective of me. They've defended me from other tigers and an acid face who wandered over here to our side of the island."

"So, I don't mean to be dense, but how can that small vial of poison help us take down Tobias? He's well-guarded, and there's no way we can get a dose of it to him," the blond lady asked.

"There's a few ways we can use it. I'm thinking grand scale - not just on Tobias. If we were to dump this entire vial in their water supply, we could take out a large number of them for about six hours. Or, we can use poison tipped arrows, shrapnel, and slingshots. This can be worked out - we can take their numbers down quickly with this formula, as long as it is by surprise."

"Right over there. There they are!"

Round-bellied Herman was leading a group of armed men towards us. The Junk Rats marched our way in a V formation brandishing their weapons.

17 JUNK RATS

"Alex, please say you did not tell Herman your plan," Mark said.

I winced.

"I spoke to him about an hour ago."

"We're all about to die," the lady in the pink dress said. "Herman is pathological. He's loyal to nobody."

The Junk Rats stepped within a few yards away. The shirtless leader, tanned with washboard abs, clenched a grenade in his hand. With a yellow-toothed grin, he slipped his index finger in the loop of the pin.

"Back up."

He stared at us as if we knew what he wanted us to do. They had the weapons, so whatever it was that he wanted, we needed to comply.

"Why do we have to back up?" I asked.

The Junk Rats formed a straight line, taking large steps toward us, pushing us toward the shoreline.

Were they forcing us to be shark food?

"What are you doing? Let's talk about this," I said.

Herman waddled up behind them, pointing at me with a smirk. His chubby cheeks were flushed, and he panted as if he had just finished a marathon.

"He's the one who was plotting against you. He's trying to betray Tobias."

My facial muscles tensed as my teeth ground together.

"Back up," the frontman said. He signaled for his line to stop. "Back up all the way to the water's edge. Now."

"Man, I don't know what kind of game you're playing, but this is ridiculous that we can't have a civil discussion."

"But you shouldn't have tried to—"

"Herman, I will deal with you later. For now, shut your mouth," I said.

Besides Larry Bateman, I'd never wanted to harm another human more than I did at that moment. There were fresh wounds on the leader's cheek, deep gashes to the bone. I had witnessed the tiger rake his claws into his face the night before. He pulled out a sniper rifle from a holster on his back and dropped to a knee, aiming it at the guard tower behind us. My mouth parched and I shuddered.

"What's in your hand, Mark?" the shirtless Junk Rat said.

"Just some chlorophyll dye," he said with a broken voice.

"Drink it."

Mark stiffened, holding the vial with a trembling hand. I gulped a painful mass of air.

"I said drink it, or I'll take a shot at the tower, and they will start incinerating you - you are all within range."

Mark threw the vial into the water and broke into a sob. The rifleman fired the weapon at the tower. A man in a blue camouflage uniform fell from the highest railing of the tower. He splashed into the water and never emerged. The Junk Rats backed up in a synchronized manner.

"Stay where you are, or I will do it again. You will be lucky if the guard tower only kills a few of you to make a point."

Mark put his fingers in his mouth and blew an earsplitting whistle. The shirtless Junk Rat widened his eyes and pointed the sniper rifle at Mark's face. The lady in the pink dress whimpered as the others remained with their feet buried in the sand, waves crashing against their calves. I raised my hands to either side of my face, palms out.

"It was me. It was all me, guys. Please, just take me with you to Tobias, and we will talk about it. These folks are innocent. They'd just threatened to notify Tobias of my plans. C'mon, let's go."

The leader shifted the barrel of the sniper rifle from Mark to me. The blond standing beside me gazed at me with creased eyebrows, blood streaming from her eyes before her eyes rolled back into the sockets. She collapsed like a rag doll, and the riptide took her body to the sea.

"What the hell just happened?"

Mark whistled again, this time it was even louder.

"Stay calm, Alex," Mark whispered.

The line of Junk Rats became restless, shouting at Mark.

"You do that again, Mark, I will shoot you before the guard tower has a chance to input your incineration code," the lead Junk Rat said.

The man beside me shrieked in pain, grabbing his temples. He crumpled to his death at my feet, nearly knocking me back into the water. There was also blood streaming from his eyes.

"What's happening?" I asked Mark. He was searching over his shoulder for something.

"It's the guard tower, Alex. Hold on, I'm calling for help," Mark mumbled.

I pleaded with the Junk Rats. "Come on, stop whatever you're doing. I'll go with you to see Tobias. It was all me."

I attempted to step toward the Junk Rats, and the leader pointed his rifle toward the guard tower with his eye against the scope, so I stepped back into place at the water's edge.

"We're standing here at the shoreline because we are in range of the towers. They are just out of range," he said, pointing to the line of Junk Rats. "They shot at the guard tower to get us incinerated. Don't you feel the back of your neck heating up?" Mark said.

My neck was a little hot from the sun, but nothing abnormal. My eyes didn't feel like they were going to start bleeding at any moment.

"No, not at all."

Mark blew an even stronger whistle, and the Junk Rat warned him if he did it again, he would be shot without delay. Two more Purgatory members fell into the water, blood rushing out of their eyes. On the side of my eye, I spotted a pair of tigers rushing our way behind the line of Junk Rats. I remembered the paw prints I had seen my first night on the island.

"Stop this. Let us move away from here, out of range. These people are innocent and don't need to die. I'm confessing, I'm alone, and this was all my idea. They were not going to betray you. These people were going to tell Tobias about my plans. Let them go, and I will go with you without a problem."

"If we let them go, you'll stay there until you incinerate."

Knowing Tony was in good hands with Mila, I would have given my life to save them, so I agreed.

"Deal."

The Junk Rats bought my story and signaled for my allies to leave. I stood in the waves, waiting for my transmitter to murder me. To give them time to escape, I pretended as if my head was hurting by grabbing my temples and bending over. Mark was the last one to leave my side.

"As soon as they get here, run," Mark whispered as he passed by.

He pressed on the sides of his head in pain as he jogged away from the shoreline. My chip never reacted to the guard tower. I glared at the shirtless leader. He cocked his head to the side and put his rifle on his shoulder, aiming it at me. He was concerned I hadn't keeled over yet. He moved the barrel of the rifle to aim at the tower and fired two more shots.

"They'll crank it up, now. You're about to fry."

The Junk Rats shouted taunts as they doubled over

in laughter. I moaned while grabbing my head to distract from the massive paws thudding against the ground. After a few seconds, two tigers took them by surprise as one pounced on the man with the rifle, knocking it into the air and slamming his body onto the beach. The other cat ambushed two of the Junk Rats at once, shoving them into the sand as he stepped on their bodies. Shrieks followed the cracks of bones as the cat rose up and tore his paws into their flesh repeatedly. Fangs sunk into the frontman's arm and the cat swished his head back and forth in a fury. The arm detached from the Junk Rat's body. The tiger threw it with his mouth, and it landed on top of the rifle. Herman snatched the unattended firearm, flinging the bloody appendage onto the ground before he scuttled toward Purgatory. A third tiger sprang from the sand at the only Junk Rat trying to save the frontman and knocked him to the ground with a ferocious growl. I spun around and caught eyes with Mark. He was waving his hands at me.

"Run!" he screamed from the edge of Purgatory.

My legs took me as fast as I could move. With the ongoing mayhem, nobody noticed me escape. Mark jogged further down the beach, and I followed him. Soon, we were out of sight.

"Mark, Herman stole their gun. Be careful, don't go after him."

"Don't worry about me, Alex."

"I'll get the numbers." He bent at the waist and heaved for air. "We've no choice but to fight now. Let's meet back here tomorrow afternoon. Follow the paw print trail to my place."

My feet tore off, and I didn't stop until I reached The Compound. A guard was waiting for me as I arrived and escorted me inside.

18 MARVIN

The news had already traveled to The Compound's leadership. Upon my arrival, I was brought to a tiny room with stale air. A round table and two chairs were in the center of the floor. An electrically powered light bulb held in a steampunk reminiscent cage swung ever so gently overhead, casting interesting patterns on the wall with shadows. Dr. Rose joined me with a pen and paper, scribbling notes as I told him about the events that had transpired. I suppose he was to report everything to Dr. Volkmann. The surgeon reasoned the chip in my neck hadn't reacted to the tower commands because it had been shorted out by the lightning strike. I was a lucky guy once again. He further explained the tower's frequency couldn't reach beyond the shoreline, and its primary purpose was as an anti-escape safeguard. However, the Junk Rats had figured out a way to use it to murder their victims in the cruelest, most painful way. This confirmed there was no hope of escaping the island. My plan to overthrow Tobias became critical to my survival,. and my determination grew even stronger.

"May I see my brother now?"

"One minute, I have one more question. Did the Junk Rats who confronted you on the beach survive the tiger attack?"

I stared at the table, trying to recall who had the upper hand when I escaped, but had no clue.

"I don't know. They were still fighting when I ran off."

Dr. Rose concentrated on his notepad, appearing to be in deep thought.

"If they survived, they'll notify Tobias of your plans. We cannot risk being associated with you until he's defeated. Your brother can stay one more night, as nobody knows he's here or that he even exists. He will be released at dawn. You, on the other hand, must leave The Compound immediately. Thank you for the information."

The surgeon rose from his seat and exited the room in haste. I shouted as he slammed the door.

"May I see Tony before I go?"

His footsteps waned as he brushed down the hall.

A guard entered a few seconds later and nodded for me to stand.

"Can I please see my brother now?"

"I was instructed to escort you from the premises."

Without another word, I marched down the main corridor and exited The Compound. I didn't want to jeopardize my brother's treatment, so I had complied without a fight.

With plans to sleep in Mila's Grove for the night, I walked toward Purgatory, crossing paths with two men who stopped short of the building – one missing earlobes and the second wearing the standard issue prison suit with two yellow stripes tattooed across his cheek. The guy without lobes was bronzed with surfer hair and a tiny pointed nose resembling a skeleton. The other boy had caramel skin and wore a fade with a stack of coiled black hair rising a few inches above his head. The disfigured lobe man was explaining what The Compound was and talking about how The Hub had recently burned to the ground. Curious as to what he had to say, I bent over to adjust my shoe in hopes to eavesdrop. He went on that it had been spontaneous combustion from dry weather and heat, but I knew the truth. I broke the ice.

"Been on the island long?"

The missing earlobe man cocked his head to the side and analyzed me as his pleasant grin morphed into a straight line. The Yellow Stripe nodded and shrugged his muscled shoulder.

"I just got here, and he saved me from those sharks, man," the Yellow Stripe said.

"Ah, yeah, someone rescued me, as well."

The blond man continued his blank stare. I changed the subject.

"Curious. What item did you choose on the ship?"

"A Swiss army knife."

He pulled it from his back pocket and shook the water out of it.

"Good choice. I made the mistake of picking a fishing pole."

We laughed for a moment, but the missing earlobe man stayed mute.

"I'm Alex Cardin, originally from Odessa, Texas."

"Marvin Frank. Houston, Texas."

"So, the yellow marks mean assault, huh?"

Marvin traced his fingers along his cheek, and then his eyes darted to my face.

"Oh, yeah, Jimmy was just telling me about all the marks. See, this kid had bothered me for years back at school. One day, I was walking home from practice; he swerved to hit my leg with his car and broke my femur. I was in the hospital for over three months and missed the entire football season. When I got out, I found him and smashed his face with a brick."

I shrugged.

"Seems fair. Was he arrested for breaking your leg?"

"Hell, no, they did nothing to him – his dad's a cop. They sped up my trial date, and I was in here before my parents could even hire an attorney."

"Sounds familiar."

Since I was in the market to recruit fighters and felt a kinship with the Yellow Stripe, I figured I would make friends instead of going solitary for the night. He seemed like a good ally to have.

"Hey, where are you guys going to camp tonight? So, you must be Jimmy, right?"

"Yes, that's right." He looked up at the sky, and the sun had begun its descent. "We'll settle in by those trees over there. There's already two fresh beds dug out. You can dig your own."

He pointed to the burrows I had tunneled for Tony and me the night before. Nevertheless, I didn't want to start trouble, so I excavated a third one for myself on the other side of Marvin. Marvin used his knife to cut off his sleeves and pant legs before he climbed into the sandy depression. A massive grim reaper holding a machine gun tattoo spanned his shoulder and trailed down his arm. Jimmy offered his bottle of tiger repellent, and I gladly accepted. However, there was something not right about him, and I couldn't get over the similar mode of operation to Larry Bateman. Saving someone from the sharks and showing them the ropes was suspicious, as this wasn't a fraternity house or a corporation. People were only friendly when they were getting something in return - altruism didn't exist on Dregs Island, or so I thought. Marvin still had on a neon-orange jumpsuit, and I wondered if Mark was just too busy recruiting soldiers to work his clothing business.

"So what's the meaning behind it? It's cool."

Marvin brushed the sand into a mound over his legs and glanced at his arm before he responded.

"Back in Houston, I was in a gang. We were all just kids, but we did a lot of bad stuff. Guess you can say I'm lucky I didn't end up here earlier than I did. Being here was my destiny."

At that moment, I regretted my decision. I was a bad judge of character - always had been. First Herman, now Marvin. There was no way to suddenly leave and then come back in the morning and wait for Tony. I didn't need enemies. I needed allies, so I was stuck for the night. With no other option, I made the best of my situation.

"How did you get bullied if you were in a gang? Wouldn't they stick up for you?"

I had never met a gangster in real life. The ones I had seen were always in movies and television shows.

"That bully kid was the boss, he ran things. That's why I put up with it for so long. We had to do what he said. To be honest, I should have red stripes like you on my face - I've more than earned them as I've probably axed over twenty folks when I was told, you know. Jimmy's taking me to meet with some dude named Toby or something. I'm gonna tell my story and see what he can do for me."

I forced my expression to remain pleasant as if nothing was wrong.

"Ah, gotcha. Well, I wish you the best of luck."

"You're one of them, right? You got the red lines on your face."

"Um, yeah, sure. I see what's going on here in Purgatory, so I can report back."

Jimmy must not have known who I was, as he never said a word and went to sleep before dark. After an hour of idle conversation about his past criminal endeavors as a gang member, the moon emerged in the cloudless sky. Soon after, we were in dreamland.

19 SNAKE ISLAND

The sunrays forced my eyes to crack open. Brushing the sand from my face, I popped upright and surveyed the front of The Compound. No Tony. The sandy beds next to me where Marvin and Jimmy had slept were empty. I must have been exhausted to sleep through them leaving unless Jimmy had instructed Marvin to sneak away quietly. In my short time on the island, I learned to trust nobody and assume the worst. After climbing out of the sandy burrow, I sprinted over to the main door and knocked. After a minute, a burly guard who reminded me of a young Arnold Schwarzenegger swung open the door.

"Your brother needs more treatment. Come back at sunset to retrieve him. And I have a message from Dr. Volkmann."

At a loss for words, I stared at his face until it became awkward.

"Dr. Volkmann?"

"He wants you to do surveillance on The Quay. Nobody's seen Tobias since the incident on the beach yesterday with the Junk Rats."

"Let me get this straight. Tony won't be released

until I spy on Tobias for Volkmann?"

"That about sums it up. See ya around sunset."

Without a solid plan, I knew I had to check in with Mark as promised. I followed the paw prints as he had instructed. Passing a cluster of poisonous trees, I carefully navigated through the brush, straining to keep sight of the paw depressions. My stomach dropped into my pelvis at the sound of tiger's snoring from within a cave. I held my breath, trying not to move a muscle until I could hatch an escape plan.

"Hello, friend," Mark said.

I exhaled with a grin on my face as if I had been given a free cupcake. Mark walked from behind the sleeping tigers.

"I thought I was tiger bait, man," I said with a whisper.

"Nah, they'll sleep throughout the day. One's nursing an injury from yesterday, and he's on some of my homemade pain remedy, knocked him out for the day. Tigers on this island are loyal and never leave an injured member of their streak. In the wild, they're often solitary. On the island, they're highly social and protective of their family."

"Their streak?"

"That's a group of tigers, Alex."

"So only one sustained an injury?"

"Unfortunately, there was one fatality, the baby of the streak."

Mark bowed his head and hunched his shoulders for a moment. I thought he was going to cry, but with his chin up, he escorted me outside of the cave to a pair of smooth tree stumps where we took a seat. The area screamed of a charming fairy tale forest with squirrels scurrying about, luscious leaves on the trees, and birds chirping. My subconscious awaited either Shrek or Prince Charming to pop out and serve us tea.

"What's the situation with you - did you speak to The Compound?" he said.

"Yes, I did. They are holding my brother captive until I report about what is happening at The Quay. With The Hub gone, there's no good way to sneak up on them. It's essentially a death mission - I'm dispensable to them, and they have leverage on me. I wished I knew where Mila was, though."

Mark clasped his hands, staring at them as if they would give him the solution to our problem.

"I know a way. Your friend Mila isn't the only one who knows this part of the island. I know all about her secret mango trees, you know. I've never interfered with her sanctuary. However, I have formed a pathway through the most treacherous part of the island. It leads to the right of The Quay. There's a great vantage point where you can see behind their walls.

"Mark, you're a lifesaver. But, it's treacherous?"

"Here," he handed me a bottle of a yellow lotion. "Put this all over your legs. We're about to traipse through a mini version of Snake Island."

"Snake Island, like that place off the coast of Brazil that was quarantined and nobody's allowed on it?"

"Yep. It's just like that. I've seen some *Bothrops insularis* vipers living there - they have some of the most potent and fast-acting venom on Earth."

I poured some of the lotion into my hand and, without question, spread it on my lower limbs. The odor was ghastly - a mix of rotten eggs and poop. I gagged, choking for breath.

"Oh, my God. What is this? Hell juice?"

"It's my formula, a snake repellent. It's the only way to survive. Believe me, many have tried. That's why nobody dares to travel this way. I've never told anybody I have this."

"It is awful, maybe the most disgusting thing I've ever smelled besides Dirty Pete's breath. No wonder the snakes don't want to bite."

"It's sulfur, naphthalene, and a few natural herbs from the island that I noticed the snakes avoid. It's about 85% effective."

"Wait. There's still a chance of being bit with this on?"

Mark's plan wasn't foolproof.

"I've never been nabbed before. I'm still standing. There are about five snakes per square meter once we get into the thick of things. Unfortunately, the last fella that journeyed with me over there got bit a few times. His skin melted off right around the bites."

"Um, did he make it?"

"Of course not. Let's go."

20 THE TOURNAMENT

Oxygen deprivation set in after holding my breath as I tiptoed through the rocky brush toward The Quay. Sparkly stars flew in front of my eyes, and I grew lightheaded as I passed by snakes of all colors, shapes, sizes. Mark wasn't exaggerating when he said this part of Dregs was like the legendary Snake Island - I had seen YouTube videos of the place, and it was nightmarish. He navigated his way as a ninja, knowing each step to take as if he'd done it a hundred times. I tried to keep up, ensuring I didn't misstep. The repellent remained noxious, but it made me safe.

After a sharp corner, there was a large, waist-high rock on the side of the trail. My body froze as I locked into a gaze with two piercing orange eyes. The snake was coiled on top of the rock, and his diamond-shaped head rose to face me. I paused mid swallow and held my breath. Mark continued to navigate the trail ahead, but I was too frightened to say a word or move a muscle. The snake's head bobbed back and forth as he sized me up, and I could hear my heart pounding in my chest. A smaller, tan snake slithered toward me on the ground, but quickly diverted his route. The repellent had worked, but I had only applied it up to my knees.

"Mark," I shouted.

The snake on the rock opened his mouth and released a spine-tingling hiss, his body forming an S shape.

"Move!" Mark screamed.

I gasped for air and raced down the trail. I may have taken flight, as I had never traveled that fast before. I approached Mark and slowed my feet.

"Please tell me we are almost there," I said as I doubled over and huffed for air.

"Buddy, you have to keep up with me."

I let out a calming exhale and shook out my hands to relieve the tension.

"I will. He just caught me by surprise."

"Look ahead at the hill that looks like a skull. We have to climb that. At the top, we'll lie down between some large rocks. We'll be able to see what's happening over there."

The creepiest looking hill I had ever seen loomed in front of us with rocky formations jutting out of the tightly packed sand.

"Should we lie on the ground with these toxic snakes everywhere? We only put the repellent on our legs."

"Alex, I'm no rookie. There are no snakes at the top of the hill – too much sun and vulnerability to hawks. A family of mongooses living in an extensive underground burrow also keep them away. They use lookouts twenty-four seven. If one dared to slither up, one of those guys would get him first."

My quadriceps burned as if acid was being poured on them with each step. Eager to have a breather from serpents, the excruciating climb was worth the pain. As we topped the hill, Mark crouched down, crawling to a spot between two large rocks. I hesitated. It felt vulnerable at the top of the hilltop as if we were on display for the island.

"They can't see us here?" I said as I followed his trail at a snail's pace.

"They've never spotted me. I come up here about once a week, just to check out if there's anything new going on in there." He pulled out an old pair of binoculars from his bag. "As long as you don't stand up and wave your arms, you're fine. Looks like they're getting ready for the ring."

"The ring?"

Junk Rats were scampering about, putting up barriers made of wood planks and barrels to form a circle. Another group arranged wooden stools and chairs around the center. I could make out what they were doing, but no fine details until Mark passed me the binoculars.

"Today must be Wednesday. It's a big day at The Quay. There are six fighters, and the strong man wins out to fight another day."

"So, six dudes go in the ring at once and go at it?" I handed the field glasses back to Mark.

"It's tournament style, all fights to the death. Sometimes, they throw a tiger in there with them if it's boring."

"Where do they get the men for the fights?

Volunteers?"

"No. They call them insurgents - anyone who gets in their way. Or, maybe because they don't like the way you look - those guys don't need a good reason."

"They called me an insurgent before."

Mark sighed and shook his head.

"Larry Bateman supplies Tobias with fighters, you know. You were with Larry when you got your clothes, but who am I to say anything? I trade for silk garments, and the Junk Rats leave me alone. They like my products, and I've never bothered them."

"Well, Larry doesn't do that anymore," I said with a huge grin. "But I think I met his replacement last night. His name's Jimmy."

"What happened to Larry? I haven't seen him in a while."

"He crossed the wrong people. Got a hatchet to the head. It was terrible."

Mark sighed. "Yeah, seen that happen too many times." He shook his head in disgust. "Alex, there are many dishonest people on this island, all trying to get under Tobias's wing. Being with Tobias was the safest place to be on this island. Until now."

After the makeshift stadium had been set, the Junk Rats of The Quay scattered into a single file line to the side of the ring. Within a few minutes, Tobias entered the area followed by four henchmen - two walked in front and the others behind him. He lowered himself into the largest chair, shaped like a throne - the back made of arrows. A minion blew a horn, and the Junk Rats filed into the space and grabbed their spots on the stools with a few shoves to move each other out of the way. Some stood behind the seated rows, forming a thick human barrier. I spotted Joe in the back row; he was taller than the rest. We couldn't discern the words, but it appeared as though the minion was announcing the fighters. Seconds later, two naked men were ushered into the ring, and their chains were removed.

"Can't we do something to stop this? I feel helpless up here," I said.

"Two men against a band of cold-blooded murderers who want to see people die in the most heinous ways. I don't like our chances, Alex."

I couldn't watch the brutality down below in The Quay. I lay flat against the Earth, shuddering at the screams and shrieks from the combatants and jeers and applause from the spectators. After an hour, the final fight commenced, and the crowd grew riotous, tossing weapons into the ring to uneven the odds. By the time the winner was declared, The Quay was in an absolute state of mayhem. Tobias never moved from his throne.

"That's most horrible thing I've ever witnessed - and I didn't even look at it. Just hearing it was terrifying."

" And that's why people want to join the Junk Rats. We, on the other hand, don't have a choice anymore. We must declare war."

"How will we do this without your poison? We've lost the advantage."

"No worries, Alex. We still have the numbers."

Down below, one of Tobias's followers ignited the fire pit. Two structures made of large tree branches and shaped into a Y flanked either side of the flames. A Junk Rat approached with a long metal rod, one side with a handle and the other with a sharp point.

"What's going on now? A pig roast?"

"Oh, no. We came at the wrong time. Let's hope it's a tiger."

Mark handed me the binoculars.

"What do you mean? We came at the wrong time?"

Two Junk Rats carried something heavy by holding on to either side of a large piece of burlap. They placed it on the ground by the flames of the fire pit. It was a human body. I could only tell it was a naked male. His light brown skin glowed ruby red as if he were badly sunburned. My heart tightened as I spotted a tattoo I had seen before. The tattoo was a hooded grim reaper with a skeletal face. It held a machine gun and spanned most of the man's arm. The man on the ground was Marvin, the Yellow Stripe I'd met the night before with Jimmy. He was dead, his face grotesque, nearly unrecognizable. I tossed the binoculars back at Mark and held my head in my hands.

"He's already been boiled," Mark said as he viewed the scene through the lenses.

"Boiled? Are you kidding me? They're going to roast this dude now?"

"They cook people, Alex. They believe eating the flesh of others makes them stronger. They boil them in a huge pot in the center of The Quay, and then bring them to the fire pit to be finished off, seared."

Nausea coursed through me like a tidal wave. I forced my eyes to the ground, still as a statue.

"Can we go now? I think I've got enough to tell The Compound to get my brother back."

"No, Alex. You don't have enough to go back to them with, but we can play a dangerous game."

"What do you mean by that?"

"I have an idea. Why don't you report what we've witnessed exactly as we've seen it? You won't be the only one they've sent here tonight, so your story will jive with theirs as if you're telling the truth. They'll believe you."

"That's what I was going to do, so what's this game you speak of?"

The men started shouting and jeering down in The Quay as the body was hoisted onto the fire pit. I turned my head away at once, my stomach lurching.

"You will return to The Compound and report to Volkmann that we were able to sneak closer. See those trees down there? Hypothetically, we could crawl through the tall grass and make it down there, but it would be an insane risk that neither of us in real life would take. If we did do such a thing, we could hear what Tobias was saying - we'd be close enough. That's the only patch of weeds that remain after The Hub fire. The other spies for The Compound can't deny that fact."

"So, we could lie and say we took the risk and went down there and heard Tobias saying whatever we want Dr. Volkmann to think he said?"

"Yes. Chances are, we won't be too far off, anyway. We should report that Tobias's planning on launching an assault against The Compound. But make it for next week, so we can give them enough time to organize and strike first."

"Brilliant. I'm down. Let's get out of here and go tell our story."

21 VOLKMANN

We trekked toward Mark's hideout, adrenaline masking my fear of snakes. Dreary clouds moved in as a distant thunder rolled in the sky. With The Quay residents in the midst of a grisly feast, and a storm lurking in the distance, Purgatory was sure to be free of Junk Rats.

"Here's the plan, I'll knock on the door of The Compound, tell the guard I have intel, we'll tell the story, get Tony, and then go back to your place to strategize."

Thunder clapped from above, followed by a dazzling display of light a few seconds later. It wouldn't be long before it was overhead. As we entered Mark's hideout, his demeanor had changed.

"Alex, I can't go with you. The storm. I must seek cover."

I was likely the only one on the island reasonably safe from a thunderstorm. Everybody else was biological lightning rods. We reached the charming forest hideout just as a few drops sprinkled down.

"Okay, I'll go solo. Wait for me here. I won't be long."

Mark went to check on his ailing tiger, and I made

my way toward The Compound as the island grew bleak. As suspected, the weather had forced everyone into structures. Thunder had roared for nearly a minute before lightning danced in the sky. The fortress was barren - not even guards poised with rifles at the open windows, as they were closed for the rainstorm. I stood under the downpour, raising my legs to wash off the stench of the snake repellent before I knocked on the main entrance. A guard I'd never seen before opened the door. I drew in a huge breath, figuring I'd have to tell my story from the start.

"Alex?" he said.

My throat constricted for a moment, and I swallowed a hard lump, brushing the water from my face with my soaked sleeve.

"Um, yes. I've just got back from The Quay. Volkmann had asked me to do surveillance."

He nodded.

"Stay right here, please."

"Wait, my brother's supposed to be released. Tony, he's in the infirmary. Can you please go get him?"

I stepped closer underneath the thatched awning to avoid the rain. A violent thunderclap shrieked, and I braced myself for what came next. The guard ignored my pleas and shut the door, leaving me to the elements. Flattened against the building by the main doorway, I waited. By the time Nurse Rose emerged, the storm had weakened. She plastered herself against the wall beside me - either hiding from someone or the rain. Either way, I sensed something was wrong.

"Hello, Nurse Rose, where's Tony?"

She waved her palm in the air and shook her head.

"I don't have long, Alex," she said in a soft voice. "They cannot know I'm talking to you. Volkmann handed over Mila and Tony to The Quay. He and Tobias signed a new treaty, but I'm unsure of what it entails. Do not trust anybody here - not even my husband." She stepped in closer to me and lowered her voice even more. "They started doing lobotomies on people for research – they're making a subservient army. They've lost their minds, and I'm afraid they may do it to me."

Upon hearing the news, my brain flickered on and off, nearly losing consciousness. I struggled to prevent my knees from locking before launching an instant state of denial.

"No, this can't be. They turned over my brother and Mila? What for? What would he possibly want with them? Mila's a girl and Tony's weakened. You're mistaken."

Thunder rolled across the sky, but it was fading and moving into the distance. The rain had dwindled into a thick, fog-like mist.

"Oh, Alex. Yes, they're gone. I can only imagine what he does with people he has no use for. Tobias's men came here searching for Mila because she was recently caught sneaking into The Quay but got away somehow. Volkmann had a sit down meeting with Tobias because he knew she used to forage for us and thought she was on a mission for The Compound. However, she wasn't – I don't know what she was doing over there, but she hasn't worked for us in the last month or so after the unfortunate incident with her friend Annie, God bless her soul." Nurse Rose paused to see if the guard's windows were open. They were still shut, so she came back to the wall and continued. "By the time their meeting was over, they were laughing like hyenas on the prowl. Volkmann threw your brother into the deal as a bonus." The door squealed ajar, and the guard snapped his thick fingers at her. The sun poked through the gloomy clouds, and the windows along the front wall of the fortress opened in unison. "I have to go. I hope you can save them in time."

"But didn't Volkmann want me to report back with my findings about The Quay?"

"Alex, it's a trap. Go now, and be safe."

Nurse Rose retreated into The Compound. I gazed at the door until my vision blurred, trying to pretend it was just a walking nightmare. After a few seconds, reality hit me. I sprinted toward Mark's hideaway as fast as my feet could push the sand. People stirred about in Purgatory, checking their huts for damage from the storm. The Junk Rat patrol would happen at any minute, so I picked up the pace and made it to the spot with wheezing lungs. I called out his name, searching for him as I caught my breath.

"Over here."

From the edge of the cave, I recoiled. The tigers were still knocked out. The streak surrounded the injured one who had been stabbed by the Junk Rats during the beach brawl. Mark was securing the last piece of tape on the cat's bandage with a huge grin spread across his face.

"How'd it go? Volkmann's going to attack The Quay now?" he said with a giggle.

I bowed my head with drooped shoulders, unsure of how to let him down.

"Not exactly. It's bad. Really bad."

His brows pinched together, eyes narrowed.

"Oh, no. Let's go chat over there."

After situating ourselves on the wet tree stumps in the magical fairy tale spot, I spewed the news in a matter of fact manner while inhaling the scent of fresh rain. His face contorted into an otherworldly grimace as he hunched forward in defeat. He removed his glasses and folded his hands together, staring into the distance.

"This is the worst case scenario." He shook his head. "I've always thought The Compound was made up of good people, non-criminals who didn't belong here. Boy, I was wrong."

The space filled with sunlight in an awkward contrast to our dreary conversation. The mist had subsided and stifling heat emerged.

"I have to save them. I can't allow Tobias to force Mila and Tony to fight in the tournament or be part of their feast."

A gruff voice repeatedly shouted my name in the distance. I froze and stared at Mark with wide eyes.

"Who's that? What do I do?"

I scrambled to my feet, not knowing which direction was best to hide.

"Stay here."

Mark slipped on his glasses as he exited his hideout from the back way. The tigers groaned from inside their cave. I had hoped they weren't waking up, as I didn't want to be discovered without their keeper there. I waited in angst on the tree trunk, and it seemed like an eternity before Mark returned with Junk Rat Joe right behind him.

"Man, are you serious? You too? Is nobody loyal in this damn place?"

Mark raised his palms and shook his head. Joe scrunched his bushy eyebrows, his face perplexed with eyes rolling in two directions as he stroked his shaggy beard. I rose to the tips of my toes, ready to take off running at the hint of an attack.

"Alex, calm down. We're going to have a talk. Joe wants to help."

The man giant took a seat on the ground by the tree stumps, and Mark lowered onto his seat and gestured for me to take mine. I peered up at the cloudless sky, pondering my collective interactions with Joe. In the Texas jail, he had been cordial for the most part - weird, but friendly. On the island, he let me escape the night of the tiger attack. But he was a murderer and a member of the Junk Rats, nevertheless, and not to be trusted. With waning options, I decided to listen and sat back down on my stump. However, I had to say my peace first.

"You were there when Tobias made those men battle to the death. They were also eating a dude I just met yesterday. Did you eat him, too? Did you cheer on the fighting?"

"No, me only eats fruits an' veggies. Me don' likes the way him makes 'em fight each other. It's not fair. Me only kills bad people who deserve it, not good people. He kills good people."

Mark interjected. "Alex, he's just one person. What did you want him to do? Fight them all and make it stop? Not going to happen."

I studied Joe's face as I gathered my thoughts. He seemed sincere. This man couldn't have been smart enough to pull off a master manipulation.

"Did you see my brother? Mila? Do you know who they are? My brother looks just like me, and Mila's a short, blond girl, real pretty."

"No, me didn't see 'em, but me left The Quay a bit ago. Me promised t'make rounds in Purgatory, but me came t' find ye, Alex Cardin. Yer my fren an' me don' wanna see ye get hurt. Jimmy was talkin' with Tobias 'bout comin' t' find ye later t'night."

My insides turned to mush at the idea of Tobias targeting me.

"You have to go back there, to The Quay. You have to save my brother and Mila. Please."

"Me no wanna go back. Thems all murderers an' I kills murderers. Too many t' kill fer one man."

I pleaded with Mark to help me convince Joe. Nevertheless, after an hour of deliberation, we had devised the perfect strategy.

"See you in a bit."

"See ye soon, fren."

22 THE BLASTS

According to plan, Joe returned to The Quay. He took over guard duty at the left side where Mila had previously charted her route to break into the area. With The Hub turned into a pile of blackened wood and charred animal carcasses, Mark and I had no choice but to hike through the Battlefield to reach the left side of The Quay. Mark brought along his usual bag of random items, but I didn't ask questions.

"Keep your eyes peeled, Alex. This part of the island can be worse than the snakes."

As we progressed, the ground transformed from loose, white powder to tightly packed sand interspersed with shells and rocks.

"I've been here once before, but only at the edge. Can't imagine how bad it gets."

The aroma of rotting bodies and putrefied fish moved into my nasal passageways after a mile of barren beach.

"And, here we are," Mark said.

We passed by a discolored human ribcage surrounded by an assortment of garbage and dead vegetation. My feet avoided seagull carcasses in a wide range of decomposition stages with stomach contents spilled out onto the ground - plastic rings, tubes, and other manmade objects among the partially-digested items. Bottles made of various materials, human bones, and crispy foliage was strewn across the shoreline, some gathered in large heaps.

"This is so gross," I said, stepping over the refuse.

"And that's why the Acid Faces are banished here."

I forcefully exhaled, holding my breath to take a break from the foul air as my feet picked up the pace.

"The smell's what nightmares are made of."

"Yeah, the clean ocean air doesn't help this wasteland." Mark paused, peeking over his shoulder with a panicked expression. "Follow my lead."

A monstrous man attempted to ambush us from behind a tall pile of rubbish. His face was severely disfigured on one side, and a glazed, lidless eye glared at us. With desiccated, yellowed skin riddled with burgundy valleys, his mouth was torn apart, teeth exposed on the damaged side of his face. His wounds were fresh, so he was new to the island.

"You'll come with me now," he said.

Mark smiled, reaching into his bag. "Let's make a deal, friend." He pulled out two palm fronds.

I recognized them as the ones holding jerky. I didn't think this would work, but I stood still, not wanting to draw attention to myself.

"Fresh food. Squirrel and rat meat. I'll give you this if you escort us to The Quay, and keep your friends from bothering us."

The monster laughed and then settled into a cold

silence, cocking his head to the side.

"I'll take you both and whatever you have in your sack will be mine. Come with me, or I'll blow the whistle. You won't like it if I do that. They're easier on those who don't resist. Your choice."

The Acid Face pulled a bamboo whistle from his pocket and poised it to the intact side of his mouth.

"I can bring you fresh food every day, and nobody has to know about it. I can even get monkey meat if you prefer," Mark said.

"I don't believe anything you say. This island is made up of liars." He stepped closer toward us. "They'll love you," he said with a finger pointed at my chest. "You're young."

Mark's plan was flawed. I surveyed the Battlefield and realized this man-beast was alone but within a whistle's blow of his allies. Nevertheless, he was isolated with no weapon in view. I went for it.

"Don't think so," I shouted as I swung my fist toward the mangled side of his face.

My knuckles smashed into the monster's exposed teeth and moved his lower jaw along with my hand. He flew backward. His body sailing back had looked like a slow motion flick. He landed on top of a mound of rubbish.

"Let's go," I said as I tore off across the beach.

We hurried through the Battlefield, dodging piles of trash and nefarious creatures dining on carcasses. Without a second to worry about trivialities, primitive survival systems carried us toward The Quay.

"Over there." I pointed to the cluster of trees I

recognized.

Last time I'd been there, I was with Larry, spying on my friend Mila. Regret consumed me as we caught our breath.

"I see Joe," Mark said, panting.

After reaching the trees undetected, we stood doubled over, gasping. Mark threw his bag on the ground, and I sat next to the tree trunk. My clothes had never had the chance to dry from the storm, but now they were soaking up copious amounts of sweat. My skin felt raw.

"Let's catch our breath before we head to the fence. Man, the hole's filled back up. We'll have to be very quiet while we dig a new one."

After a brief respite, we crawled on our bellies to the fence line. Joe acknowledged us, giving us the okay to commence the dig. The soil was soaked and still soft, as they hadn't packed it down. It didn't take long for us to crawl through to the other side, but we were covered in wet sand and muck. We crouched down and hurried toward the wall.

"Now what? How do we find them without getting caught?" I said.

Our plan wasn't well thought out, but we were modifying it as we went. Joe pretended to fidget with his shoe and pointed an index finger toward the back of the Quay at the shoreline.

"Ah, he did mention the enclosures were by the beach," Mark said.

Hunched over, we trekked toward the ocean. With sweat pouring from my pores, my final step brought me to the end of the wall.

"There."

I pointed to a row of bamboo cages.

Mark whispered as softly as he could. "There's a serious problem. We'll be exposed beyond this wall. How the hell can we get over there?"

About fifteen manmade enclosures spanned the backside of The Quay. Piles of dead people filled the pens. The bodies were unnaturally posed and overlapping as if each had collapsed to their death. My heart lurched inside of my chest.

"The storm. They were left out here in the storm. They're all dead." Stricken with a gruesome fear, my eyes searched the cages for familiar features. "I don't see either one of them though."

"Me, neither, but some are facing the backside or at the bottom of the mound."

"Psst," a tiny voice whispered from behind. "Hey, you. Thanks for re-digging the hole for me, saved me a bit of trouble."

I spun around, expecting to see a Junk Rat. It was Mila.

"What are you doing? I thought you were being held prisoner here? You're working for them now?"

She smiled and cocked her head to the side.

"No, not at all. This was all planned. Well, besides your brother and now you showing up here. If you Cardin boys would just leave it to the professionals," she giggled.

"Where's Tony?"

She grabbed my forearm and pulled me back from

the wall's end.

"We're working on that. He's next in line for the boiling pot, but I have this handled."

She was calm in an unnerving way. I gulped, but no words came out.

"Alex, you okay?"

Her eyes begged me to respond. My brother was in line to be boiled to death, and a panic overcame me that put every nerve I had in my body on fire. I found my voice.

"What? Are you kidding? Let's go save him."

I didn't want to wait. I thought there was no way I could stay hidden behind a wall when my younger brother's life was at risk.

"Be patient, friend. Trust me. Go back to the trees outside of The Quay. It's good you're here. Tony will need your help. You'll have a two-second window once it all goes down."

"Alex, you should trust her. Let's go," Mark said.

Unsure of putting my trust into a girl I'd been around a handful of times, Mark and I crawled our way back toward the hole. A few times, I nearly gave up the plan and ran to save Tony, but Mila seemed like she had this worked out. Joe signaled for us to make our move, and we hurried toward the fence, scooted underneath, and then huddled behind the cluster of trees.

"What do you think she meant when she said this was all planned?"

Mark lifted a shoulder, shaking his head. "No clue. I'm obviously not a great strategist, and I've never been good at reading women."

Smoke plumed from the center of The Quay. My insides quivered, muscles clenched.

"Please say that's not the boiling pit fire."

Our eyes remained focused, waiting for a sign. Minutes passed, and I grew restless. I was a second from making a move toward the main entrance to offer a switch for my brother's life. In hindsight, that would have been a terrible idea – Tobias was nowhere near honorable and would have just put me behind Tony in line for the pot.

"That's not the pot fire. The Quay's on fire, Alex."

Mila, a Junk Rat, and Tony rushed around the wall and hurried toward the hole in the ground. They snaked their way underneath the fence, shouting for us to follow them. The Junk Rat reminded me of a Hollywood actor with hero hair and a strong jaw. He had perfect features as if drawn by an artist. His bright white teeth were not something you would see on everyday people.

"Mila's Grove. Don't stop, don't look back," she shouted, leading the way.

Mila reeked of an accelerant as she whooshed by. Tony's eye was shades of purple, and his lip was swollen. Shirtless, he still wore a bandage on his back, albeit it was covered in filth. His strong will to live kept him agile and able to keep up with her.

With a quick glance over my shoulder, I smiled as The Quay morphed into chaos, Junk Rats scampering about as they fought the spreading fire she had set in the supply shack. As we tore off toward the

Battlefield, two Junk Rats spotted us and rushed through the main gate.

"They're coming after us," Mark said.

Mark was older, and not in the best physical shape. He fell to the back of our group as our feet pounded the sand, moving our bodies at top speed. It sounded as though a thunderclap hit right behind us as a massive fireball shot up from the middle of The Quay. Fiery balls of yellow flames exploded into the sky followed by plumes of dark, thick smoke rising and merging with the clouds. After a full body shudder and gasp for air, I pressed on, forcing my legs to run as three more blasts went off in succession.

"There go the weapons," Mila huffed.

Mark shrieked. He had fallen far behind.

"We've got your friend." An unfamiliar voice shouted over the ruckus as we moved toward the first wave of junk piles of the Battlefield. "Stop now if you want him to live."

Another blast erupted from the center of The Quay with shrapnel soaring away from the epicenter.

"Don't stop. Keep going," she said.

The others didn't miss a stride as they sailed across the carcasses littering the ground. My feet slowed as I turned around to see the two hostile Junk Rats seizing Mark by the throat and yanking his arms behind his back.

"Don't even look back, keep going," our Junk Rat friend said.

"He's my friend. I can't leave him. Let's fight. There are only two of them."

"Wrong. There are four now, and more are coming," Mila said.

I slowed down once again, and our new ally stopped and grabbed my arm. He swung me in front of him behind Tony, pushing me in the back to run faster.

"More are coming, Alex. They shouted for back up. We'll get Mark back. Keep running. You won't do him any favors being dead. Your brother's safe with us now, remember that. They won't kill Mark. They need him as leverage."

In a streak of good fortune, we sped through the Battlefield unnoticed by the Acid Faces. By the time we passed The Compound and entered Purgatory, I was struggling for air. I caught eye contact with one of Mark's allies who had been on the beach the day Herman betrayed me. He narrowed his eyes as he surveyed our group. I assumed he wondered why Mark wasn't with us.

"Do not slow down now, Alex, we need to hide. Mila's Grove," she said as she took the position behind me.

Tony stumbled. The Junk Rat behind me lunged to steady him, and held Tony's arm while he increased his pace.

"You okay, bro?" I asked.

Tony nodded, but I could tell he wasn't doing well.

"Maybe we should stop for a minute, Mila?" I said as I gasped for air.

"Almost there, Alex. Push forward."

As soon as we drew near the poisonous trees, Tony

collapsed onto the ground.

"Tony? Tony, you alright?"

23 GUNSHOT

Tony was out cold, but still breathing. I looped my arms under his shoulders, pulled him up, and carefully navigated between the Evil Queen Trees into Mila's Grove. Our new ally helped me lift him into the hammock. My brother was soaked in sweat, and his face was as red as a strawberry. In true Hollywood spirit, Mila's new friend seemed as if a stylist had prepared him for the next scene in the movie.

"I'm Gabe."

"Alex." We shook hands with a firm grip. "So how'd you meet her?"

"She's a born leader, a fierce judge of character. She knew I was an innocent the moment she saw me."

I'd have thought the same if I had seen him – virtue seeped from his skin. Mila examined Tony, checking his cheek for fever as he swayed gently, still sleeping.

"He'll be fine. Nurse Rose said he was out of danger of infection," she said. "He's just been through an ordeal since he's arrived. I don't even know when he ate his last meal. I'll grab some fruit and, when he gets up, we'll get some food in his stomach. Don't wake him - he needs rest, or he may die of exhaustion – I've seen it happen."

She was about to head to the mango trees when I spoke.

"What did you mean by all of that being your plan?" She halted in her tracks and spun around to face me. "You were betrayed and traded to Tobias this morning, right?"

A roguish grin spread across her face, her eyes twinkling with mischief.

"I orchestrated the whole thing. In exchange for your brother's medical care, I agreed to remain in Volkmann's debt, knowing he'd eventually double-cross me and trade me to Tobias. I killed Larry in front of the guards to ensure they'd release me as a forager - they have a firm policy on violence and make no exceptions for *guilty* murderers. Didn't realize they'd tattoo my face and give me the mark, but whatever – there's no beauty pageant here."

I stared in disbelief before I responded.

"Strict policies on violence, yet they sell humans for slaughter and give people lobotomies in hopes to create a submissive army to fight for full island domination. I'm high from the hypocrisy," I said, shaking my head. "But how'd you know you'd meet Gabe?"

"I didn't. That was the gray area of the plan, but I knew there were plenty of people in The Quay who don't belong there. I knew instantly I could trust him. He released me from the cage before the storm hit, saved my life."

Of course he did. I mused. They traded smiles, and he winked at her.

"What should we do now?"

I followed her to the mango trees while she picked a few. She passed one to Gabe and me, and handed us each a knife from her bag.

"Nurse Rose told me she could recruit over half of The Compound to our side. She has all the guards in the front and all of the patients in the research program who know they're about to be lobotomized and can even get more. We just have to give her a signal, and can't allow Volkmann or her husband to find out about the plan. It needs to be quick. If the evil duo catches on, it's over, and her life is in grave danger."

"Wait a minute. Nurse Rose knew about all of this? Why didn't she say anything to me this morning?"

"She lost her marbles over Tony. They'd grown close during his stay - she misses her son so much, you know. But they blindsided her, and she had no clue Volkmann would hand him over to Tobias. That wasn't supposed to happen, that wasn't even in the deal. Natalie's lucky to be alive after the fit she threw. Her husband was enraged at her behavior, and they got into a vicious fight right in front of Tobias and Volkmann."

Slicing my mango, I replayed my conversation with Nurse Rose from that morning.

"Ah, yeah, she warned me about her husband. She's worried he'll harm her." The thought of losing our top ally hit me. "Oh, man. We've got to get over there before they scramble her brains."

I slowly raised a piece of mango to my lips, my

mind racing to formulate a strategy to save her.

"We should organize first. How many do you have?"

Gabe and Mila both removed their shoulder bags and plunged their hands inside. They pulled out grenades and handguns and lined them up on the ground. I cupped my hand over my mouth, gasping.

"Wow, you've thought of everything."

"Not everything, Alex. Our plan was to get all of their weapons, but we needed a distraction to save Tony."

"Dang, sorry."

She lifted her shoulders and dropped them back down.

"No worries, we take care of our own."

My brother hadn't budged, and the swinging bed had stopped moving. His chest rose and fell with deep breaths, and his coloring had morphed to a soft pink.

With time working against us, we left Tony to rest and set out to Purgatory to gather Mark's allies I had met. We explained our strategy to each of them including the plans to overthrow Tobias, Dr. Volkmann, and to save Mark. After a couple of hours, we had over two hundred people standing beside us. The army wasn't as big as we'd planned, but many people didn't believe we could take over Volkmann, and some thought we had betrayed Mark. I was about to address the new recruits as a voice rushed up behind me. I recognized the voice and trembled with anger.

"I see what you're doing, and I'm going to tell Tobias right now."

Herman was holding the rifle he'd stolen from the Junk Rats on the beach. He obviously wasn't comfortable with the weapon, as he struggled with putting it on his shoulder. He only had one hand and wasn't physically fit, to say the least.

"Tobias will probably give me a residence in The Quay when I turn you over," Herman said with a smirk.

A few members of our group gasped and moved to the side.

"Herman, put the gun down. You don't want to do that. Tobias is about to be overthrown, and The Quay will be under our control. Don't you want to be on the right side of things?"

I stalled, trying to think of the best plan to disarm him as he fumbled with the gun's position on his shoulder. I was reasonably certain he wouldn't hit me with a bullet if he fired the gun, but not sure enough to bet my life on it.

Mila stepped behind me and whispered into my ear. "When I give the word, duck."

"Just ally with us," I said. "Join us now, and you'll be taken care of in the new society. Fight us, and you'll be sorry you didn't."

Herman's face morphed from anger to uncertainty as if he were controlled by another force. He started to put the gun down, but then hoisted it back onto his shoulder, peering through the scope as he pointed the barrel at my chest.

"I should shoot you right now, Alex. Tobias would be so happy. I'd be rewarded, probably get a month's worth of shark meat."

Herman fought with the weight and bulkiness of the gun. I felt movement behind me, so I tried to keep the stall going.

"Herman, you should realize that Tobias is not going to be in power long—"

"Move," Mila said.

I lunged and dove to the ground as an earsplitting blast rang out, the aroma of gunpowder peppered the air. An unwavering tone pierced my brain. Our new soldiers groaned as they clutched the sides of their heads. I shook my head as I scampered to my feet.

"Get the gun," Mila said.

Herman's eyes widened as he dropped the rifle and grasped his chest. Blood soaked through his silk shirt, and he crumpled to the ground.

"On it." Gabe rushed over and picked up the gun, hoisting the strap around his shoulder.

"To The Compound," she ordered.

24 ALONE TIME

Two guards were waiting for us at the entrance. They signaled for Mila to approach them. The rest of us stayed on the side of the building to remain out of sight. However, it was a challenge to keep two hundred people quiet, especially since many of them were psychologically unstable. A man started an argument with himself about the size of coffee grounds in an imaginary filter, while a silver-topped man couldn't stop kicking a tree trunk. He swore it was bugged by the government and would relay our plans to Tobias. For all I knew, the man was right, but I did my best to quiet him and prevent him from hurting himself. Gabe worked hard to mediate the argument over coffee grounds.

A few minutes later, she popped her head out of the doorway and commanded us to storm the main fortress. As we moved into the corridor, we were instructed to obtain a weapon from the guards. They had a limited amount of guns, an assortment of knives and various other heavy objects. In a single file line, we entered the foyer. We were told to spread out like opposing magnets, in a branching treetop pattern, detaining and silencing anyone who opposed us.

"Dr. Volkmann's a short man, not much taller than me. He wears blue-rimmed glasses and is balding. He has frizzy white hair and a recessed chin. Find him first."

"What do we do with him?" a female soldier asked, after accepting her handgun from the guard.

Mila continued to address the group as they piled into the main entrance. "Shout as loudly as you can for back-up if you spot him. Also, be on the lookout for Dr. Rose – he's taller, dark-skinned with big ears that stick out. He'll probably be in scrubs. Once you have assistance, tie their hands, and bring them by gunpoint to the lab suite in the east wing. I'll be in there. Once we have them, the people here will have no choice but to listen to what we have to say. Do not allow these two men to manipulate you or promise you anything – they are not to be trusted. They're intelligent and will try to outsmart you to save themselves."

A man with a metal baseball bat raised his hand as if he were in a classroom. Mila nodded.

"But what are you going to do with him in the lab?"

"There are prison cells there. Ones he had built for his unwilling research subjects. I'm going to free them right now. I'll meet you there."

I was offered a revolver. The metal was cold to the touch, and my hand felt natural on the handle. I'd never shot a real gun before but had played enough virtual reality video games to feel somewhat confident. Before I pushed off, I inquired about the safety. The type of gun I was holding didn't have one, and the guard told me to be careful. A second guard whispered, "Godspeed," to each of us as we passed by him. Some turned right, and the rest veered to the left.

"Please let me find Volkmann," I mumbled, storming down the corridor. "I owe him one."

Feeling more alive than I ever thought possible, I opened every door and inspected every corner of each room as if I were the star of an action thriller. Random shouts and shrieks rang out from the fortress as dissenters against our cause were detained. I marched into the infirmary suite, a place I recognized. Nurse Rose was in there, sitting on a chair in the middle of the largest room with dim lights. Something wasn't right.

"Are you okay?" I asked as I took a step into the room.

She remained still, quiet, her hands folded on her lap. Her puffy, reddened eyes nudged to the left. I took the hint and slammed the door toward the wall with my shoulder, knocking the surgeon onto the ground. He had been preparing to ambush me had I taken one more step, as he held a full syringe in his clenched fist. I kicked his hand, whacking his weapon across the floor. By instinct alone, I shoved my gun into his mouth.

"Do it, Alex. If you don't shoot him, I will!"

Nurse Rose stood up and walked toward me. My hand danced lightly on the trigger, but I couldn't force myself to kill him. I was unable to pull it back. With muffled pleas, Dr. Rose begged me not to do it, sweat pouring from his face. He heaved for air as he wrestled to remove the gun barrel from his mouth. I pushed it in further until he started gagging. This wasn't me. It wasn't in my DNA to kill another person – no matter what the reason.

"I've got this," Nurse Rose shoved me out of the way and grabbed the handle of the gun. She bent over to face her husband as he squirmed on the ground. "I have dealt with your physical abuse for far too long. I overheard you talking about your plans with Volkmann last night. I listened to every detail of the plot to lobotomize me and hundreds of other innocent people. How could you? Your plans to build an army of brainless soldiers is over – and so is your life." She sobbed as she pushed the gun further into his throat. "Alex, look away." After Dr. Rose launched a muffled cry for help, she fired the weapon, and a high-pitched blast exploded inside of my brain. "Don't look. You don't need to see that. Let's go get Volkmann. I know where he'll be hiding by now."

Her voice sounded as if it were coming from a remote overhead speaker. I took her advice and tore my eyes away from Dr. Rose and lunged over to pick up the loaded syringe. We raced down the corridors, passing by our soldiers who were working hard – some escorting rebels, and others recruiting new members.

"No turning back now, huh?" I said.

"You can say that. I won't feel safe until the other monster's behind bars – or better yet, dead." We turned a sharp corner and entered a narrow, dark hallway. "He'll be in here." She checked the gun for bullets and found three more. I held the syringe with caution, as I had no idea what was loaded inside of the barrel.

She pulled out a set of keys from her pocket, resembling those I'd unearthed in The Hub. Tobias must have made that part of the deal with Mila and Tony. *Glad I helped.* She sorted through the keys and crammed one into the lock. It twisted clockwise until it clicked, the door latch snapped open.

"Dr. Volkmann, it's over," she said as she stomped into the room.

The space was large, filled with lab benches and cabinets that held an array of vials and bottles of liquids and powders. Vintage machinery and tools were strewn out across the tables, connected by wires and tubes. Composition books with scrawls of data were scattered on the tabletop. A couple of stools were knocked over - a sign of a struggle or quick escape.

"Dr. Volkmann. It's Natalie Rose." She checked every cabinet to ensure he wasn't hiding in them. "Dr. Rose's gone, The Compound's collapsing. It's over. You can come with us peacefully or die. Your choice – you know which I'll prefer."

After searching every nook in the room, we concluded he wasn't there. A skinny door in the back caught my eye. She crept over to it with the gun, and I stood by the side of the door with the syringe's needle pointed toward it, my thumb on the plunger. If whatever was inside of the syringe was good enough for my veins, I figured it was tit for tat if it ended up in Volkmann's. I spoke to the door.

"This is Alex Cardin. You gave permission for my life to be saved with the antitoxin, and you saved my brother. For these reasons, I will ensure your safety. But you must come willingly. You're going to be locked up, but we will keep things humane."

My heart skipped a beat as the doorknob twisted. I readied the syringe, holding tightly with a sweaty palm. With a slow, grating creak, the door opened. A tiny man stepped out with his hands raised on either side of his face. He donned blue glasses, and his hair was a white ball of fuzz – just as Mila had described.

"Your plan is futile. Tobias is too strong. He'll defeat you. Don't say I didn't warn you," Dr. Volkmann said with a thick German accent.

"Don't listen to him."

He was half my size, so I tossed the syringe on top of a lab bench. We exited the room with the gun pressed against his temple.

"I will make you my confidant. You can stay here, in The Compound. You and your younger brother. I will speak to Tobias, and you will have immunity from The Quay for the rest of your days on this island."

We pushed out of the cramped lab. I held his arm with a vice grip. Nurse Rose gazed into my eyes as we escorted him down the hallway.

"Don't listen to a word he says. He's a demon, pure evil. Over a thousand people on this island have died from his hands. He's insane and needs to be locked up for good."

The thought of living protected in The Compound with my brother was tempting for a half second. However, I wasn't stupid. I realized he was only trying to manipulate me.

"Sorry, doc. You'll have to live your days in the jail cells you built. At least you'll live a better life than your research subjects will. You have Mila to thank for that."

The chaos in the building subsided, and more civilized rumblings filled the air. We pushed into the lab suite and joined Mila who was unlocking the last prison cell. The lab was bigger with modern equipment. There was an open room with a surgical table in the center. Narrow doors lined the back wall and down a long hallway where more doors flanked both sides.

"Not that one. Please leave that subject in his room. You don't understand, please do not release him," Volkmann said.

Volkmann struggled to exit the room, but I held onto his arm, pulling him back toward me. Nurse Rose, still holding the gun to his head, threatened to pull the trigger.

"Face the music, Volkmann," she said.

Mila opened the door, and a massive, muscled man with tattoos of demons and dragons across his chest came out of the holding chamber and into the lab suite. He had two red stripes on his cheek and a series of whelps and rosy spots across his abdomen. I assumed those were from whatever this mad scientist had been doing to him.

"Where's the knockout gas, Dr. V? You forget to strap me down to the table? How are you gonna torture me now, little man? How are you gonna jumble up my brains with the drill like you promised?"

Upon hearing his words, I scanned his head and saw a small circular scar between his eyes. The man marched across the room and grabbed Volkmann by the front of his shirt. We released our hold on him as the angered man tossed Volkmann's frail body onto the surgical table as if he were a bag of feathers. He begged for his life, but his pleas fell on deaf ears. Nurse Rose headed for the door with a huge smile on her face, and I followed.

"Let's give them some alone time," Mila chuckled.

25 THE AMPHITHEATER

Volkmann's screams rang down the hallway. The plans to incarcerate him were quickly abandoned with his research subject's impromptu retaliation. We walked the halls of the fortress and found many of our men and women escorting the mutineers to the prison cells. Others were communicating Mila's mission of creating a new society, and people seemed receptive. Our strategy was working.

"I'm going to ring the bell and call a meeting in the amphitheater," Nurse Rose said.

"Wow, you guys have an outdoor theater here? This place is amazing."

"It's still rather primitive and was already here when Dregs Island was made into a prison. Rumor has it that there was an isolated tribe that lived here once upon a time. Oh, and the US military used parts of the land for storage and whatever else, who knows."

She grabbed a megaphone from a wall niche and announced her meeting as she strolled down the main walkways. I followed the herd toward the theater, ending up behind the coffee ground guy. He was speaking to a woman about how well the mission went, and how happy he was to see the island make these changes. I suppose his argument about the sizes of coffee grounds had been resolved.

As I exited the back of the fortress, my eyes laid upon a wide-open courtyard. It was beautiful, with trees and picnic benches spaced throughout. In the theater, a wooden stage centered at the bottom surrounded by ascending lines of rock slab seats. Confused faces gathered as they walked down the aisle and filled the rows, sitting down in a stupor. We had changed their lives in less than an hour. They had the right to be perplexed. Mila assigned a team to be on the lookout for Junk Rats in the front of the fortress, and to perform a thorough sweep of the grounds to account for everybody. The people of The Compound were civilized and waited patiently for further instruction. After about ten minutes, our soldiers gave the signal, and she addressed nearly a thousand people from the stage using the megaphone.

"Greetings. I already know most of you, but my name is Natalie Rose, and this young lady standing beside me is Mila." Many faces smiled, some nodded, and a couple of folks balked about the red stripes on Mila's face. However, most stared forward in a vacant oblivion. "The Compound has fallen." The audience chatter ceased, and many exchanged mystified gazes. "Dr. Volkmann and Dr. Rose are gone." Gasps, groans, and soft rumbling sounded. One person started a clap and recruited many others, eventually building to a subtle applause. She continued. "There will be no more living in fear. This facility will now be used as a prison to detain dangerous criminals on this island. We are going to bring forth a new society. We are going to treat people who need help – both mental and physical - to the best of our abilities. We will restrain murderers, pedophiles, arsonists, and rapists behind bars where they belong. We will turn The Hub into a much-needed farmland. We will tranquilize and capture the tigers and use them to guard our new prison facility."

Mila held her hand out for the megaphone, and Nurse Rose surrendered it to her with a beaming smile.

"We have a long and dangerous road ahead of us. We will soon face Tobias and his merciless followers, but we can do this. We have the numbers. We have the weapons. We have the intelligence. We can summon the necessary aptitude and become fighters for a cause, and take over this island to make a new civilization. The society we create will be fair, impartial, nurturing, and it will guarantee safety for all upstanding citizens."

A full round of applause erupted as people began to rise and cheer. After a few minutes of hugs, praise, and smiles, the audience took their seats and hushed. A man in the front row broke the silence.

"For the last six years, we've been unable to defeat the Junk Rats. We're simply not murderers. We're bankers, lawyers, teachers, and even some ex-members of the clergy. Half of Purgatory's looped out of their minds and won't be able even to pick a side to fight for. You speak of weaponry? What? A handful of guns with a limited amount of bullets and some metal pipes?" He threw his hands in the air, trying to sway the audience members around him to his side. "Do you know how many of those crazed killers are in The Quay? Have you done the math? If that doesn't convince you this is a fail, this will. I heard they found a bunker full of military grade weapons. I applaud your spunk, but you ladies have lost your ever-loving minds. When Tobias hears about what's happened here, we're all goners. Thanks, girlies, you've just signed all of our death certificates, hope you're happy."

Exaggerated moans and prattling filled the amphitheater. People rose from their seats. Mila gestured for them to sit down.

"Please listen, everybody. He's sensationalizing, and I don't blame him, I'd do the same if I were sitting on your side. We're all on edge, uncertain of what's ahead," Mila said with a calming voice. "However, I can tell you what we've done thus far, and maybe you'll start to trust that this plan can work." She waited for the audience to silence and the last few people to take their seats. "I'll address each one of your concerns, sir. First, you say we're not murderers, so we're automatically outmatched. Military members weren't murderers before they enlisted, but they kill their foes to make the world a better place. We're no different. We'll use our brains, charm, and intuition to turn our enemies into allies. If that fails, we capture and contain. Only as a last resort will we utilize capital punishment – but that'll be their choice, not ours."

"You spoke of the people of Purgatory. You're right, that's where many unstable people live. However, there are far more people there who aren't crazy that would love to see this place have social order. Those people took over The Compound, the most fortified place on this island with the highest educated minds. Don't underestimate or discount them." She was interrupted by a spirited cheer and applause. "Yes, sir, we've done the math. Our army outnumbers The Quay now by three to one and that's being conservative. And your last concern was about their weapons. I blew up their weapon supply house, but stole what I needed along the way." She dipped her arms in her bag and then brandished a grenade in each hand. Mila and Nurse Rose exchanged proud smiles as they received an extended standing ovation. Gabe smiled at Mila from off stage, and she blew him a stealthy kiss.

The silver-topped soldier who had been kicking the tree trunk earlier entered the amphitheater and rushed toward me.

"There's a Junk Rat asking for Alex. Isn't that you?"

"Yes."

I waved and signaled the stage that I was headed to the front with the silver-topped man. They nodded and acknowledged me.

"What do you think he wants? Do you think he knows we've taken over The Compound? Do you think he's here to ambush us?" the silver-haired guy said.

After turning the corner and entering the main corridor, I caught a glimpse of Joe peering into the window as the rifled guard warned him he was going to shoot.

"He's not here for an ambush," I said to the man walking with me. I rushed over to the guard as I shouted. "Don't shoot, he's a friend, Joe, meet me at the entrance down here." I pointed which direction to go, pushed down the passageway to the entrance, and instructed the guards to let him inside.

His face was mystified as he stroked his shaggy beard and entered the foyer.

"Me heard the speech. Ye took over this place, an' me's happy. Tobias knows, though. He's got spies who tell 'em what's goin' on."

I sighed but figured that would happen sooner than later.

"Where's Mark? Is he alright?"

"He's at The Quay. Me took 'em from the cage an' hid 'em in me secret place o'er there. We gots a bit o' time b'fore they can spot 'em. Me had t'act likes me was foraging fer food t' leave. Me couldn't bring Mark with me."

"Understood. Alright, go back and don't raise suspicion. Just watch his back, and keep your eye on Tobias. We'll be there soon enough."

Joe nodded. "B'careful, Alex." He hurried outside.

By the time I got back to the amphitheater, the audience was disbanding, all in high spirits. I sprinted to the stage and approached Mila and Nurse Rose.

"How'd it go? Everyone seems happy."

"Great. Half of the folks are going to stay here and prepare prison cells - making them out of existing rooms and reinforcing them with padlocks and so forth. They're also going to make temporary holding cages out of bamboo. It's going to be a mess while we organize the place," Mila said.

"And what are the other half doing?"

"We're taking down Tobias and his followers. Today. He probably knows we've taken over this place, as he has eyes and ears everywhere. I'm going to recruit more fighters in Purgatory, and then we're heading out. Oh, go check on Tony. See if he's woken up. He'll need to get some food in his stomach. Meet us in the center of Purgatory in ten."

Today seemed too soon, but I quickly agreed with her point of view. She had no other option.

"Joe was here. You're right. Tobias knows what we're doing."

"I figured. News travels fast on this island, huh?"

I nodded my head with a smile, promising to meet back in ten.

26 CHAIN-LINK FENCE

With the recent storm, the air was muggy. I was unsure if my damp clothes were from my sweat or high humidity. I passed through the poisonous trees and into Mila's Grove. It was stifling inside of the hideaway. No breeze. The hammock was empty and still. My stomach knotted.

"Tony!"

There was no sign of him anywhere. I searched the area, shouting his name. He was gone. I tore off to find Mila, my eyes darting from side to side.

"Tony!"

I screamed his name repeatedly as I ran, looking in every nook and every window. My eyes scanned the branches overhead and the ground surrounding tree trunks. I made it to the middle of Purgatory as Mila was finishing a speech. I waited while holding my breath, my eyes searching for Tony among the faces.

"How's our sleeping prince? Still asleep?"

"He's gone. I can't find him anywhere. Do you think Tobias has him?"

I huffed for air, pressing on the stitch in my side.

"No way. My place is secure. It's not possible that a Junk Rat would go near a patch of Evil Queen Trees right outside of snake city. They're not real smart, but they all know not to do that."

"But what if he woke up, got confused, and left? It was extremely humid in there - hard to breathe."

"Well, now that's more of what probably happened. He could have left and got lost. Or, he could have run into a pack of Junk Rats - we know some were here spying on us. Time is ticking, though. I've just recruited about three hundred more people, maybe more, but I don't want to give them time to change their minds. We're about to invade The Quay."

"That's not enough. We're supposed to have at least three to one - that's what you promised the people of The Compound."

Mila shushed me and pulled me a few feet away from whom she had been addressing. She lowered her voice so that only I could hear her.

"I miscalculated, but we have enough, don't worry. I'll have some men scour Purgatory and look for Tony. I'll also send guys to double check The Compound."

"If we don't find him?"

"Let's not assume the worst scenario. We leave in five. Here, you'll need this."

She tossed me a hand grenade with a smile. I flinched as I caught it. It was far heavier than it looked.

"Hey," I shouted.

"It's not armed, silly. When you use it, yank the pin out, toss it toward your enemy, and run. Haven't you seen any war flicks before?" She smiled. "Go help find your brother."

My legs went into perpetual motion and took me through Purgatory. I went in between each hut, looked in every window. I asked everybody I came into contact with if they had seen him. I searched every inch of where he could have gone. Tony was nowhere to be found. I returned to Mila's Grove one last time in hopes he had just been climbing a mango tree. He wasn't there. The only places he could have been were mini Snake Island, the Battlefield, or The Quay, and all options were ominous possibilities. With defeated spirits, I made my way back to Mila. Purgatory was packed to the brim with people, and I had to push my way through to the front.

"He's not here."

I lowered my gaze to the ground.

"Alex, don't fret. He'll turn up. The quicker we overthrow Tobias, the quicker you don't have to worry about Tony, as he'll be safe on this island."

Mila stepped up on the porch of a hut, directing her newborn army to gather. Rough-and-ready soldiers – both men and women - filed in close and silence arose.

"It's time to overthrow Tobias and create law and order on Dregs Island. This is our home, and we're about to make history. Today will be perilous. Some of us may give our lives for the cause. I'm prepared to die for a new civilization where people don't have to live in fear, are you?"

Applause erupted with boisterous cheers. She had

gained their trust, their loyalty. It was too difficult to count, but with a crude estimate, I believed we had nearly a thousand people by the time we strode toward The Quay.

"As we travel the Battlefield, if any Acid Faces make trouble, warn them first, give them a chance to retreat, and if they do not - end them," Mila said.

"So, what's the master plan?" I asked as I marched alongside Gabe and Mila in the front of the group. Nurse Rose had stayed back to manage The Compound.

"Okay, Alex. We've got twenty-two soldiers with guns. I don't believe The Quay has any firearms, as there were only grenades, bombs, and rocket launchers in the military bunker - and we blew up their storage. If the Junk Rats had guns, they'd be using them during their patrols, but they don't."

"I've seen one with a rifle, though. The one Herman tried to use on me."

"That may have been their only one, and we have it. If they had guns, they'd all be armed when they left The Quay."

"So, they could have a few grenades, rocket launchers, or bombs. Great."

"I doubt they do - they're not the most intelligent people on the island - they probably stored the whole lot together."

We navigated our way through the trash piles in the Battlefield. There were a few Acid Faces that came to see what was happening, but they retreated behind the mounds of refuse and didn't choose to confront us.

I shuddered as a gunshot rang out from the back of our formation.

"Guess that one didn't want to back off," Mila said.

Gabe laughed.

"Once we get to The Quay, what do we do?"

"Storm the entrance and spread out once we get inside of the fence - just like we did in The Compound. Give the Junk Rats a chance to join us or retreat before we take them in as prisoners. If they fight us, they die - but it's their choice. We kill Tobias - no delay and no questions asked. With the crimes against humanity he's responsible for, he doesn't deserve to live. We've gotta make a strong example out of him, so we don't get a Tobias part two. I have a feeling, with him dead, the Junk Rats will surrender and fall in line with our new society."

"You think it'll be that easy? They know we're coming."

"We don't have a choice, do we? If we stay on our side of the island, they'll attack us and have the upper hand. No, thank you."

As we neared the final hill before The Quay, my heart pulverized my chest cavity. The front line had grenades in hand. The gunmen were directly behind us. The rest of our warriors were armed with syringes filled with tranquilizers and other sedatives, knives, swords, and various blunt objects. I didn't know what to expect when we got to The Quay - an awaiting army in formation, an ambush from either side, or maybe even a white flag. We reached the top of the hill, and a vice grip tightened around my heart. My lungs seized as my eyes locked with a horrific sight.

"Holy hell," Mila said.

Two bodies were strapped to the fence on either side of the main entrance, both of their faces bleeding profusely. It was Mark and Tony. Without saying a word, my legs took off toward The Quay.

"Don't. It's a trap, Alex," Mila shouted.

I didn't care what she said. My brother and my friend were in danger, and I was going to rescue them. Wearing blinders, I wanted to save them at all costs. Once I reached the fence, I scaled it high enough to release Tony's ankles – they had been bound with rope and tied to the chain-link.

"They're going to kill us all. You need to run," Mark said.

"Go, Alex, get out of here," Tony said.

Peering over my shoulder, I was surprised that our army wasn't rushing in behind me. Instead, they retreated to the other side of the hill. I was alone. With one grenade.

"Where are they? Why's nobody here guarding you?" I asked.

Mark shrugged his head toward the left and then toward the right.

"They went both ways. They're hiding. I suppose they're waiting for your army."

I scaled higher and untied Tony's right wrist. He moaned as the rope released, scarlet streams trickling down his arm. His face was puffed up, riddled with gashes.

"Mila withdrew our army."

I freed Tony's left wrist and helped him climb down the chain-link.

"Go catch up with Mila. She's on the other side of that hill. I'll get Mark," I said to Tony.

Tony complied. As he sprinted toward the hill, arrows flew out from either side of The Quay, one striking him in the leg and the other in his shoulder.

"Run!" I screamed.

He stumbled as he got to the top of the hill, and then disappeared.

"Poison arrows," Mark said. "We're sitting ducks."

"I have to help Tony. I'll be right back. I need to see if he's okay."

"They will shoot you, too, Alex. Don't be a fool. If Mila's on the other side of that hill, she'll take care of him."

I hesitated, trying to scan the area to see where the Junk Rats were hiding. I couldn't see any of them, they had hidden themselves well. Mark was right. I figured if I was to be of any help to Tony, I had to be alive.

"Alright, I'll get you down, and we'll go inside of The Quay. We have to do what they don't expect. Maybe we can make our way back to the shoreline and swim to another part of the island?"

I climbed the fence and untied Mark's legs.

"Sharks in the water, Battlefield on the left, and Snake Island without repellent on the right. Not going to happen. I'll take my poison arrow for the win."

After I unraveled the ropes restraining his arms, we

scaled down and scurried inside of The Quay.

27 THE DECOY

As we hurried through the Junk Rat sector, everything was a blur. I anticipated the pain of being struck by poison arrows. To my surprise, the only thing aching was my quadriceps as I beat my fastest running speed. As we reached ground zero of the explosion Mila had ignited, we slowed out of curiosity's sake.

"She caused some damage here. Took out a few of their guys too."

Charred human carcasses were strewn out as if they had been tossed in the air during the blast. The main storage building in the center of The Quay was in pieces, blackened, and full of ash. Many of the surrounding structures were also incinerated and in shambles.

"Love the way they take care of their dead, huh?"

I scanned the area. Counting bodies, I got to twelve. Not enough to make a difference.

Mark shook his head. "In there." He pointed to a dwelling, reasonably built with a few burn marks on the front where the explosion had reached it.

"Hope nobody's home."

We entered a cabin, and the aroma of cedar and

perspiration struck me as peculiar. The residence was far more structurally sound than the shambled huts in Purgatory. A tiger pelt was spread out on the floor by a small fireplace filled with ash. A wooden plank bed held a handmade mattress and blankets made of Mark's silk.

"Not too shabby, huh?" I said.

"Nope. So what do we do now? Wait until someone comes to kill us?"

"I have this."

I raised my grenade in the air, and he pressed his lips together in thought. During the silence, an image of my brother lying on the ground on the other side of the hill popped into my head, and I suppressed a panic attack. After taking calming breaths, I willingly entered a state of denial and convinced myself that Mila had taken care of him, and he was fine. Tony was smart – or at least I needed to believe that to make it through the next couple of hours.

"There's a cut-out there."

He gestured at the window in the front of the cabin with poorly crafted blinds.

"When we see them coming, we take them out with that. After the blast, we run outside and steal the weapons of the dead and dying, and come back in here for cover. Then, we are set."

"That's the only plan we have, so we'll go for it. I'll take first watch," I said.

I dropped to my knees, weapon in hand. With minimal blinks, I watched for Junk Rats. After a few minutes, heavy footsteps pounded the sand outside the cabin. With a finger, I nudged the slat to get a better view and locked eyes with Joe. He was standing among a group of Junk Rats that were searching the grounds.

"Don' see 'em," he shouted. "Not in Tobias's house, me checked in there. All's clear."

More Junk Rats infiltrated the area, and I ducked, gesturing for Mark to do the same. We scooted toward the wall behind the door in case anybody entered the cabin. Our plan was failing, as I wasn't able to use the grenade with Joe standing there.

"We're in Tobias's house?" Mark mouthed the words. "It's almost dark. He'll find us."

I nodded, searching around the space. After spotting a bag in the corner, I crawled over and retrieved it. There were packets of palm fronds filled with jerky. My hands wrapped around cold metal at the bottom of the bag. A switchblade knife.

"Score," I whispered.

More Junk Rats emerged but started to scatter about The Quay - no doubt on a hunt for Mark and me.

"Guess Mila retreated all the way back to Purgatory," he whispered.

"Maybe so. Let's scoot back, out of sight of the doorway. The only chance we have of survival is to surprise."

I gave Mark the explosive and held on to the knife. Over an hour had passed before we heard more footfalls. With a massive surge of adrenaline, I crouched into position, waiting to pounce on whoever came through the door.

"I will rest now. We attack at nightfall," a deep voice boomed on the other side of the door.

An iron fist clenched my heart as the door creaked open. My pores unleashed sweat droplets all over my body. With white knuckles, I gripped the knife with clammy palms, conjuring visions of my brother being struck with arrows to give me courage.

Tobias stepped into the cabin and swung the door close. After two steps inside the room, I leapt from the corner and tried to slip my arm around his thick neck. With the strength of three men, he grabbed my shoulders and flipped me over his head, slamming me into the wooden planks of his bed.

"You think you're man enough to fight me, boy?" he snarled, gripping my throat with his enormous hands, his muscles flexing their might as my throat tightened.

I struggled for air, trying to release his grip.

"Acid Faces are at the gate!" a voice outside of the cabin screamed.

The room blinked into blackness, my chest heaved. My hand combed the bed for the knife I had dropped.

"Everyone, to the gate at once!" a different voice sounded from outside.

With my index finger, I pushed down, sliding it toward me until my fingers could clutch the blade of the knife. I worked my hand toward the handle, and he squeezed my neck with all his might, nearly closing my windpipe.

"I have a grenade. I will pull the pin and will blow

us all up right now," Mark said.

Tobias was unfazed by him. He knew he was bluffing, but it was enough of a distraction for me to jam the knife into his chest. After slicing through his flesh, I used my palm to push the handle in as far as it would go. Choking from his vice grip around my neck, I fought for breath.

Black silence came next.

"Wake up, Alex."

With one hazy eye, I made out the silhouettes of Mila and Gabe. My body was halfway on the wooden bed, the edge of the board pressing into my back. My throat was tight, sore. My neck stung as if I'd been burned with a blowtorch.

"Where am I?"

Unsure of how much time had passed, I opened my other eye and tried to focus. Bamboo walls, tiger pelt, fireplace, and a pool of blood on the bed next to me, oozing toward the floor. I was still in the cabin. I found it difficult to move my neck around to survey the room but was relieved that Tobias was gone.

"How many fingers am I holding up," Mila said.

I cleared my throat and choked.

"Three."

"Who am I?"

"Mila."

"You're a hero, Alex."

I sat upright, forcing my diaphragm to inflate my lungs to their maximum capacity. Struggling to remember as I dealt with sharp pains shooting through my chest, I pieced together a vision of pushing the knife into his heart. Then, nothing.

"Where's Mark?"

Gabe held out his hand and pulled me to my feet. "Mark's safe."

"Tony! Where's Tony? He got shot with—"

"He should be fine. He's with Nurse Rose, getting the arrows removed and treated with antitoxin."

I endured the most painful exhale before choking. Each cough radiated surges of agony through my body, and my throat constricted. I wanted to shout for joy, celebrate, but gasped instead.

"He squeezed you pretty good, Alex. We'll have Nurse Rose examine you, but I've seen a few people get choked out, and they're usually alright," she said.

Mila opened the cabin door. The sky was hazy, and it was nearly sundown. An organized pandemonium was underway as our soldiers marched rebellious Junk Rats into the cages - the very pens they had used to house tournament fighters and victims of cannibalistic feasts. I beamed at Tobias's body displayed on a chair in the middle of the blown up storage house. The knife was still in his chest; blood trails had covered his torso. A large X was drawn on his forehead in blood.

"Yep, we did it."

Mila smiled, and Gabe gave her shoulder a soft squeeze with a grin.

"How? I thought you retreated?"

They both laughed.

"What? Are you serious?" She laughed. "No, we

outsmarted. One thing about battle – you never do what they expect you to do." She stopped to give instructions to Joe and other members of the army before she continued the walk toward the front of the complex. "You took off, playing into their hands to rescue Mark and Tony. We back-tracked and went to the Battlefield to recruit and regroup."

"You allied with pedophiles?"

Mila put both palms in the air to calm me.

"Not exactly. We just offered them a deal many couldn't refuse."

Gabe glanced at her, wanting to take over the story. She smiled and nodded.

"I found the leader in the Battlefield – by the way, that place is wretched," Gabe said.

"Yeah, it reeks," I said.

"It gets worse the closer to shore. I'm unsure I'll ever smell right again."

Mila stomped her foot against the sand with a smirk.

"C'mon, tell the story, or I will."

She swung open the gate. As we passed through the fence, we stepped over bodies dispersed around the entrance, all with arrows jutting out of their flesh. All of them were Acid Faces.

Gabe continued. "I asked the leader if he'd gather some of his guys to help us defeat Tobias."

"And he said yes? It was that simple?"

"The guy realized we had a big enough army. He listened to our story and confessed he hated the Junk Rats more than we did. Tobias has done some pretty terrible things to them."

I sorted my thoughts about Gabe's story as we hiked up the hill toward The Hub. We walked in the open, and it was nice not to have to sneak around anymore.

"I started to sympathize with them," Gabe said. "Many expressed remorse for what they'd done in the past. Many didn't want to live in the Battlefield with the trash, and carcasses, and told me they'd rather die than spend another day living with guilt from their crimes."

"They died for the cause?"

Mila gave a slow nod with a cautious grin.

"Well over a hundred Acid Faces willingly sacrificed themselves for the new society. As far as the remaining ones, we'll integrate those who deserve it, like the innocents and guys who fought for us and survived, and we'll imprison the others," she said.

A pit grew in my stomach for the ones who had perished. Gabe raised his hand to signal he would continue the story.

"They stormed The Quay while the rest of us made our way toward the left side. Junk Rats never saw us coming, as they were busy with the Acid Faces. We followed the fence line all the way to the shore and ambushed them from the back. Our first wave was a grenade launch, and then, we took out the rest with gunfire. Tobias was our only wild card – but you took care of him, Alex."

Mila smiled at me, and Gabe gave me a friendly smack on the shoulder. The trees of The Hub were barren and blackened, like a Tim Burton film set. Our shoes turned black from the slag on the ground as we marched on top of the loose soot, kicking up a cloud around our shoes like a storm cloud. An unnerving aroma of burnt steaks on a grill engulfed me as we passed countless animal carcasses among the heaps of ash and burnt vegetation. I made out most of them as monkeys, tigers, birds, and an array of rodents. We reached the peak and took a moment to take in the island from the highest point. Without lush trees and canopy blocking our view, we scanned 360 degrees around the shoreline. The island was a beautiful place, a paradise, or at least it was going to be.

28 JAMESTOWN

Eighteen solid days had passed before we could say we had a judicial system. We had secured the prison population of Dregs Island as humanely as possible. Overcrowding seemed to resolve itself, as the prisoners made it a habit of killing one another if we put any of them together in the same space. The remaining Junk Rats had fallen like dominoes. Many of them proclaimed innocence and filed into the new society without issue, and the others who resisted were issued a jail cell. Mila and Nurse Rose had assigned a crew in charge of erecting a stronger, permanent facility. It would be at least a year before that building was ready.

Mila and Nurse Rose performed day-to-day inspections of the island and coordinated with appointed committees on how to proceed with improvements. I often tagged along on their walks through town, as I had been appointed as city manager. Tony was in charge of food and agriculture, but we both took on various jobs in addition to our main duties.

"President Mila, you're doing a stellar job," I said as we strolled through what we now called

Jamestown.

"Alex, you tell me that every day, and thank you. And, I've asked you not to call me that."

She giggled, squeezing my arm.

"What will your people refer to you as?" I laughed. "Princess Mila? No, Queen Mila has a nice ring to it."

"I don't need a title, man. I'm just going to manage this island as a healthy civilization should be run. Checks, balances, punishments for crimes. They can all call me Mila."

The area was bustling with people remodeling and building new structures under the direction of the architects and structural engineers of the former Compound. Musicians played various instruments made of bamboo, sharkskin, and coconuts on a stage in the center of the town. People created road signs and were putting them up on the newly formed thoroughfares. I joked around and requested an *Alex Cardin* street. The following day, there was a sign for it on the main pathway going through town.

"I can't believe we did it," Nurse Rose said.

I grinned at her.

"If it weren't for you, we'd still be hiding out in Mila's Grove eating mangos, trying to hide from Junk Rats."

"Alex, you are far too kind. We all know it was a collective effort," she said with a chuckle. "You arrived on this island, and six days later, Tobias was history. That's no coincidence, my friend."

We strolled by Gabe. He was in charge of the judicial system. He was standing in front of a group of recruits lecturing on how to patrol, take care of the tigers guarding the new prisons, and how to handle firearms. It was awesome to witness a law enforcement division being built from the ground up.

"I see he's got a new batch," Mila said.

"Gabe's been busy interviewing almost everybody on the island to recruit the best officers for his team. I'm so proud of him. We can sleep safely at night because of him," Nurse Rose said.

"I believe we can truly be happy here, you know. Everything is falling into place," Mila said as we walked upon Mark who was busy working on his silkworm farm expansion.

"Mark wants to expand his clothing business and build a small factory. He's pretty excited," Nurse Rose said.

Mark and Natalie had grown close and were about to open an apothecary that would sell herbs and medicinal treatments. She planned to set up a clinic right next to the store. Nurse Rose held up her hand and paused in front of Mark's hut.

"Have you had a chance to find suitable containers for the snake repellent?" she asked.

Mark stopped grinding mulberry leaves and set down his mortar and pestle on his workbench. He strode toward us as he straightened his glasses.

"Ah, Natalie, yes, I did. I collected hundreds of small plastic bottles from the old Battlefield and cleaned them out. They'll work nicely. We'll launch a recycling program to get the empties back once we open for business."

Nurse Rose grinned with a nod.

"You're so resourceful, Mark. Can't wait for the guys to finish building the store - I've got a team collecting all the herbs I need to make pain relievers and antitoxins."

Mark saluted Nurse Rose and smiled.

"See you later, Natalie. Bye, guys."

"Bye, Mark," Mila said. "After we inspect the rest of Jamestown, let's check on Tony at the farm, I haven't been out there for a few days. Do you know if anything has sprouted yet? I know he was very worried the soil was too burnt to be fertile."

"Not that I know of, but haven't been there today," I said.

Enjoying the fresh salty air and gentle breeze, we trekked to the Cardin Farm.

"I see the lightning center is nearly finished," I said.

We passed by a large building that was still under construction. The structure was to be a storm shelter for the residents. Nurse Rose vowed to figure out a way to remove the neck chips, but until then, the island residents needed a safe place to be during the lightning storms.

The sun was still ruthless, but Mark had made us all sunhats, which were a blessing. We climbed the hill toward the farm. Tony and I had removed the ash and burnt vegetation from The Hub and brought over mulch from mini Snake Island. Using seeds we had found in the former Compound, we planted an entire fruit and vegetable farm under the direction of a landscaper that had been sent to Dregs for tax evasion. Each day, we watered the ground with collected rainwater, waiting for shoots to pop out. We had plans to build an irrigation system but didn't want to waste time on it if the land was infertile.

"Hey, Tony," I said.

He held a rake and had an enormous smile spreading across his face.

"We got sprouts!"

We rushed up the hill and walked carefully between the rows of planted seeds. He was right. There were a few whitish stalks with bright green leaves growing above the soil. Mila and Nurse Rose cheered and clapped, congratulating us.

"Wow, that's amazing. What's this row?"

"Mustard greens, I believe. And over there, carrots shoots are emerging."

I noted the position of the sun in the sky.

"Now let's hope the rest of the seeds follow suit. Tony, look at the time, gotta go."

"That time, huh?" he said, placing his rake by the row of mustard greens.

"I'm ready for some beach time," I said with a laugh.

Mila snapped her fingers as if she had remembered something important.

" Ah, guys. Gabe met a fishing boat engineer during his interviews for the police force. When he discovered the man's old occupation, he asked him to reinforce your canoe. I believe he took care of this late last night since that shark dented the side of the one you were using," Mila said.

"Cool. Yeah, we had a close call a couple of days ago while saving a serial killer. Go figure. We should just let the Red Stripes try to make it to shore by themselves," I said.

"Well, you two boys arrived on this island as Red Stripes and were innocent of the charges filed against you. Never forget that," Nurse Rose added.

"But that crazy dude tried to kill us with his ninja stars as soon as we got to the beach," Tony said. "If it weren't for Joe, we'd both have new star ornaments protruding from our foreheads."

We doubled over in laughter.

"Alright, ladies, we're heading out for rescue duty. We'll see you at dinner," I said.

29 MOTHER'S LOVE

The sun shone brightly on our pair of lounge chairs. We lowered ourselves into them, ready for duty.

"Anybody arrive yet?" I asked Joe.

Joe had been assigned as the full-time beach guard. His job was to maintain order and control of the shoreline around the tube to ensure nobody made it to Jamestown without our knowledge.

"Nope, it's been quiet. Me's enjoying the waves. Me likes the slow days."

After a few minutes, a man walked onto the edge of the tube.

"Alex, we got one."

From the shore, I could only make out a pudgy man, probably middle-aged if not older, not very tall. I grabbed the binoculars. The dark receding hair and black-rimmed glasses struck a memorable chord, but I couldn't place where I'd seen him before. He was a Red Stripe.

"That guy picked something real small. He's holding it in his fist."

Tony accepted the lenses from me to get a better view.

"Man, he looks so familiar. You ready?"

It bothered me for a few seconds that we both had the same thought of the man. I shrugged it off as we ran toward our newly reinforced canoe and dragged it into the water. A large ship with red and blue flashing lights sped toward the island, and we exchanged mystified looks, grabbing our paddles. Since my arrival, I had yet to see a boat of any kind besides our manmade canoes. We had concluded that the military personnel in the towers must have lived there, as we never saw anyone come and go. The tower guards had been quiet since we took over the island. We assumed as long as we didn't bother them, that they had no problem with what we were doing. One night, we all admitted and agreed we liked having the towers there as a sense of protection from outsiders.

The stout man plummeted toward the ocean, and we paddled toward him with a life preserver in hand. Within a minute, we were close enough for a rescue, and his head popped out of the water's surface. He wasn't a strong swimmer and struggled for air. As if an invisible person slapped me in the face, I remembered this man.

"Tony, the same judge that sent me here, sent you here, right?"

"Yeah, same guy. Glasgow."

"That's him. That's why we recognize him. That is Judge Glasgow."

I threw the life preserver toward him.

"Ironic, huh?" Tony said as he kept his paddle down in the water to steady the boat.

"Yes, it is. He'll go straight to a prison cell for what he did to us. We'll talk to Gabe and have him skip the due process."

"What do you think he did?"

"Probably killed someone else with his death mobile and couldn't find someone to frame for it," I said.

A large dorsal fin passed by the judge's face.

"Hurry and grab the float, and we'll pull you in," Tony said.

Judge Glasgow locked eyes with us. The panic faded from his face as his mouth went agape and eyes narrowed. Treading the water, his head bobbed at the water's surface. He gazed at the life preserver and paused. He shook his head slowly and waved a palm above his head in a gesture for us to go away. Another shark fin joined in, circling him. He started to sob.

"I'm sorry. I'm so sorry for everything I did to you boys. I'm a very bad person," he shouted as he opened a small red glass vial and consumed the contents. It was a bottle of cyanide from the item wall. "They'll explain." He looked back at the ship that was approaching. "I've left everything I had to you."

He lifted his arms and sunk into the water.

"Grab the life preserver," I shouted at him.

A shark burst out of the depths with the judge's leg inside of his mouth. He swam away at the surface with the judge bouncing against the waves. Then, the shark dove deep, and we never saw the judge again. The sirens from the ship grew louder, and a PA system crackled.

"What the hell just happened?" Tony said.

We sat in the canoe without a word as the large vessel with flashing lights came closer. The speaker cracked and hissed before a voice came clear.

"This is Captain Harold Alan from the United States Navy. We are here for Antonio and Alexander Cardin."

Tony and I sat still, staring at each other.

"What. The. Hell," Tony said with widened eyes.

"Not a clue."

Without thinking, I waved at the ship from our canoe.

"Alex, what if they're here to kill us?"

"Nothing will stop them until they get what they want. They will kill innocent people if we try to evade them. Plus, you still have a functional chip in your neck. You're in the range right now - they can use an incineration code on you at any moment."

"Good point."

They sent a roped ladder down to us, and we climbed aboard. Armed officers aimed their guns at us.

"Great, we're gonna die for making Jamestown," Tony mumbled.

"You are Antonio and Alexander Cardin?" a pale young man in a navy sailor suit asked.

Once more, we confirmed our identity. The suited man used a mechanism to scan the chips in our necks. Mine was unreadable, but they further verified who I was by a finger prick blood test and DNA analysis. Once we were identified, the commander of the

United States Prison System walked up to us, identified himself, and shook our hands. He had the appearance of a Marvel comic book character, like Superman, the all-American hero.

"On behalf of the United States of America, I hereby offer you both a formal apology." We both exhaled. I breathed in a breath through my nostrils until I almost passed out. My contracted muscles relaxed one by one, and I shook out my limbs, smiling so hard my cheeks started to ache. Tony and I grabbed each other for a tight embrace. The commander cleared his throat. We released each other and nodded. "It has come to our attention in the matter of the State of Texas versus Alexander Cardin, and the State of Texas versus Anthony Cardin, that there were grave injustices that occurred with both of these cases. You will both have your marks removed immediately. We have a laser on the ship and a renowned dermatologist who's the best at removing ink from skin. You'll attend a debriefing when we reach Houston, but I wanted to personally notify you that your family will be taken care of by the US government for everything that has transpired."

From around the corner, my mother rushed toward us, shrieking. She seized my hand, her eyes welling up at her lower lids.

"Alexander."

She paused, staring at my face for a long second before throwing her arms around me. We held each other for a long minute, her floral perfume whisking me away to my home in Odessa, Texas. She pulled away and kissed my forehead, gazing at me with love in her eyes, still gripping my hand as if I were holding on to her at a cliff's edge.

"Mom, did you do this? You got us out of there?" I asked.

She released her grip and took a step back, her face swollen from crying, but she smiled brightly through her reddened eyes. During the twenty-four days I had been on the island, she'd aged years. Before she responded, she threw her arms around Tony. She pulled him in for a loving hug and then kissed him on the forehead. After taking a step backward, she held out a hand to each of us. I gave her my hand, and she clasped it tightly.

"You are the first ones ever to be released from a prison island. You're free, all charges dismissed." Her voice trembled with emotion. Choked up, she paused to catch her breath. "This has sparked a full investigation of the new laws involving felonies across the nation. They're reviewing all cases within the last six years of people being expedited to the various islands. They've created a national committee made up of the top legal minds to investigate a more secure and fair reformatory system. They will probably reopen all the prisons back home. Many of the prisoners will be released immediately back into society. The system had always worked, it didn't need to be changed."

I smiled at her, grabbed her by the shoulders, and pulled her in for a bear hug. Tony wrapped his arms around both of us. We sobbed together, but it was blissful.

"I love you, Mom," Tony said.

I stepped back and gazed into her eyes.

"You're an incredible woman."

I turned to the commander.

"Can we say goodbye to our friends on the island?"

"Alex, no! You don't want to go back there," my mother said.

"I would highly advise against returning to the island, Alexander. We cannot afford to risk any of our officer's lives by giving you an armed escort. However, if you wish to ignore my advice, we will wait here for you - we owe you that. Please realize, you will return to the island at your own risk," the Marvel character commander said.

"One more thing," I asked. The commander nodded. "There's a girl. Her name is Mila, but I don't know her last name. She has already been on the island for three years for a senseless crime. It's bad enough you guys took her hand."

The commander stared at me with blank eyes.

Tony stepped closer and tugged on my shirt. "But what about Gabe, Mark, Joe, and Nurse Rose?" he whispered into my ear.

I turned to him and whispered, "Let's don't push our luck. They'll all be released soon."

"Is there something else you need, Alexander?" the commander asked.

"Also, there's a nurse, Natalie Rose. She was sent to the island for a silly reason, and has done more than her share of time. We would like to have her released, as well. Would you consider allowing them to ride back with us to the mainland?" I asked.

The commander stood silent for a moment. He retreated into the cabin of the ship with Captain Alan without saying a word.

"Argh. We asked for too much," I said.

Tony looked at me with wide eyes and shrugged a shoulder. My mother stepped in front of us with tears in her eyes.

"Alexander, Antonio, I beg you just to go home. Please do not return to that dangerous place. I couldn't live with myself if something happened to you."

Over the next ten minutes, our mother tried to convince us not to return to the island. She eventually understood the situation and why we couldn't leave without a word to our allies. The commander returned with a smile on his face.

"Alexander, you may retrieve Mila Cooper and Natalie Rose. I must say again, you'll be doing so at your own risk, without an armed escort."

"Are you sure you want to do this?" my mother asked.

"Mom, I promise you. We'll be okay," I said.

30 THE REFUSAL

Tony and I climbed down the rope ladder and jumped into our canoe. We paddled toward shore.

"This is an insane turn of events, huh?" I said.

"Can't believe we asked to go back to the island," Tony laughed. "But we couldn't leave like that. They'd always wonder what happened to us. I'm sure Joe saw us climb aboard the ship. I'd hate for them to think something awful happened to us."

"I know, it just felt wrong. Let's gather everybody around and give the news."

Joe was waiting for us on the shore. He helped us drag the canoe by the trees.

"Them the feds? They angry at us fer changin' the island up?" Joe anxiously stroked his beard.

"No, it's all good. We need to go find the girls. We've got some great news for them," I said as we trekked through the sandy trail toward Jamestown.

We promised Joe we would come back and tell him the news after we delivered important information to a couple of people. He agreed. After an exhilarating march through town, we caught up with Mila and Nurse Rose in the middle of Purgatory by the live band.

"You will never believe this, Mila," I said.

She wore a befuddled smile.

"Nurse Rose, you will be so happy," Tony said with a huge grin on his face.

"What are you two so cheery about? Something happen on the beach?"

Tony and I exchanged glances with big smiles.

"Our mother singlehandedly had these islands declared as unconstitutional. They are all being abandoned, and the old prison system will be reestablished. All cases will be reviewed. Many of the prisoners here will be released into society back on the mainland."

Mila and Nurse Rose stood motionless with wide eyes. I thought they would have been happy, but neither of them seemed to enjoy hearing the news of their pending releases.

"But, what if we don't want to leave the island?" Mila asked.

"Well, I haven't got to the best part, Mila. You and Nurse Rose can come back with us on the rescue ship. The commander said he would take you two back to the mainland, and your cases will be reviewed first. You'll both be free," I said.

Gabe approached and stood behind Mila.

"What's going on?" he asked.

Mila turned solemn as she turned toward him.

"It seems as though Alex has bargained for Natalie and my release from this island. They want to take us home. Right now."

A tear streamed down her face as Gabe wrapped

his arms around her.

"You should go, Mila. We may have come a long way here with Jamestown, but this is still a prison. We can't leave. We're trapped here with dangerous people, and we have these chips in our necks."

Nurse Rose cleared her throat and stepped closer, taking my hand in hers.

"I respectfully decline the offer to leave the island today. This is great news, as I'll be able to reconnect with my son one day, but I'm just not ready to do that right now." She bowed her head, and a lone tear hit the sand below. "I murdered his father on this island. Many may agree it was justified, but I could have locked him up, and we both know that."

"Nurse Rose, he was a terrible man. He—"

"Alex, you are the sweetest, but I don't think my son would ever forgive me for what I've done. I could also end up in prison back home, and that would be dreadful. I just need some time to sort through these feelings." She squeezed my hand and smiled. "I have so much love and respect for you and Tony and feel this is the right option for both of you. Get back on that ship with your mother, go home, and live your lives to the fullest. Jamestown is my home. Mark and I have great plans for the future on this island. I wish you both the best of luck," Nurse Rose said. She gave me a hug and then gave one to Tony before she walked away with tears in her eyes.

Mila and Gabe gazed at us with mystified looks on their faces.

"I agree with Natalie." Mila clasped her hands

together and stared into the distance. "This island is my home. I'm happy here. Even if you were to bargain to bring Gabe back with us, I'd still want to stay. If this is all true, and the government is going to reform the justice system again, I'll accept them removing the dangerous prisoners on the island. I'll allow them to remove the chips from our necks, or at least deactivate them, so we don't have to fear lightning as much. But I will fight if they try to put an end to Jamestown and force us to leave."

She stared at me with determined eyes. Tony and I exchanged knowing gazes.

"Mila, I will make it my mission to ensure you get to stay. I have a story to tell the American people. My mother has already shown what she is capable of, and once she hears of your wishes, I'm sure we can figure out how to make this happen. Maybe they'll even consider Jamestown a tourist spot one day? We'll come back for a vacation."

We all laughed for a moment before exchanging embraces.

"We thank you for everything, Mila. Gabe, you take care of her," I said.

"Not a problem," Gabe said as he cradled her shoulders with a smile.

"Guess this is goodbye," Tony said.

Mila smiled. "For now."

ABOUT THE AUTHORS

The authors are a mother and son writing team from Austin, Texas.

Dr. Bon Blossman is an award-winning fiction author and founder of the world's top murder mystery game company, MyMysteryParty.com. She is also a recording artist, a developmental physiologist, and former college professor with nearly twenty years of teaching experience. Dr. Bon completed her Bachelor of Science in Pre-Medicine, her Master of Science in Biology, and her Ph.D. in Developmental Physiology before completing a postdoctoral fellowship in a developmental cardiovascular research program. Dr. Bon is also in a band (DrunkLora) and writes short films for her company, Little Ghoul Productions.

Zakk Myer is a psychology student at The University of Texas at Austin. He is also a music producer and musician, playing various instruments such as the piano, drums, and the bass guitar. Zakk is currently a member of an indie rock band, The Other Kids (soundcloud.com/otherkidsmusic). Zakk has also produced music for various projects, such as Dr. Bon's book trailer for Blood Dolls. Zakk has plans to graduate from UT and pursue a career in music and film production. He co-founded the film production company with Dr. Bon (Little Ghoul Productions).

Made in the USA
Middletown, DE
31 January 2020

83994760R00151